QUANT

kylekeyes.org

KYLE KEYES

PRELUDE

Jesse Joe Jacks was born sometime during the snow blizzard of 1923. The Lower Elk County, game warden died from a lightning strike on July 23, 1959.

Olan Chapman came to life in August of 1974 and found a computer career with a center city, electronics firm.

Jacks loved nature and lived to protect wild life. Jacks was also a crack shot with a firearm - any firearm. Chapman attended the theater, played piano and at one time led a march against the National Rifle Association.

Jacks fought in the Korean Conflict and never drank anything stronger than beer. Chapman fought a war from within, and never sipped anything lighter than scotch on the rocks.

Both men had the same fingerprints.

KYLE KEYES

QUANTUM ROOTS
The Vigilante Sightings

Plots and characters that form this storyline are fictional, as is the weather. Public Domain and fringe area details are true. All storyline names are fictional, and any resemblance to persons living or dead is purely coincidental.

There is no FIC (Federal Intelligence Center), and any descriptions or procedures described here-in, may or may not correspond with the whole, or any part of our national Intelligence Community (IC), which encompasses the FBI, CIA and a changing number of other intelligence agencies.

There is no Lower Elk County in the state of New Jersey.

Product name usage is not an endorsement by author, publisher or printing house.

Quantum Roots is founded on the belief that particle energy formats with quantum root systems that can bypass time and space. This is not science fiction.

KYLE KEYES

QUANTUM ROOTS

Dedicated to Danny

CHAPTER 1

"Olan Chapman!" cried wife Ivy, "Slow down!"

"I'm not speeding," replied her husband, "It's this weather. Bad weather creates an illusion that telephone poles and other objects are flying by faster than they really are."

"Olan, that's bullshit."

"Actually, the objects aren't moving at all," said Olan Chapman in slurred tongue, "It's the car that's moving."

"Thank you Albert Einstein," said Ivy Chapman.

They fought verbally as they barreled through driving snow, and weaved wildly between oncoming cars, A snow plow loomed from no where and the bony computer geek slid onto the blurry shoulder to let the giant steel scraper pass by. Chapman cursed this early season storm and went on to say, "I really wasn't ready to leave, Ivy."

"I think you had enough to drink, Olan."

"Ivy, the party was just getting started and if you would drink something beside carrot juice, you might fit in better, and I wish you would stop counting how many drinks I sip."

"I think you mean guzzle," said Olan's bride of seven years, "Normal people sip. You guzzle."

Christmas lie twenty days ahead. Dead Man's Curve waited ten minutes down the road. Numerous parties would highlight Lower Elk County over the next few weeks. The Carson City Bridge was out. Thus, all who traveled from Mt Loyal City to Hobbs Creek were detoured to a snaky back road left over from horse and buggy days. Olan and Ivy Chapman were now among that number.

"And I wish you would stop telling everyone that my first name is Poison," continued Ivy Chapman grabbing an arm rest, "People do not find you funny and I think you just side swiped that pickup truck."

Screeching brakes and broken glass sounded as a red four by four spun a one-eighty, and ran head on into a green sedan that broadsided the next car in line, which led to one huge pile up.

"And why would you ask for Rye Crisp," said Olan Chapman peeking in the rear view mirror, "I can not believe you asked for Rye Crisp at a cocktail party. Rye Crisp is not an appetizer."

"I don't like those little slimy things," explained the dieting Ivy Chapman, "They reek with a fishy odor."

"They are supposed to smell fishy," said the bony computer geek who grew up in a ivy covered mansion and graduated from a Buffalo university "They are fish."

"And the creep with the giant penis?"

"That was not a real penis," said Olan, "That was just a balloon made to look like a penis."

"That was not a balloon," said Ivy, "It was a dildo."

"It was a balloon."

"Olan, I know a dildo when I see one. That fat bastard screwed the girl over the back of the sofa with a sex toy."

"He did not really screw Lucy," explained Olan Chapman, "He only pretended to screw her."

"Olan, he had her pants down to her ankles and he was pumping her from the rear," said Ivy, "I know when a girl is getting screwed."

"It was just in fun."

"Olan, you're drunk," said Ivy, "You abhor sex unless you're drinking. Then you go from a Jekyll to a Hyde and that whole incident was not amusing."

"Well, it was Looney Lucy's idea," replied Olan, "And I'm certainly not going to step in. Harold is one of our senior members. Not to mention, he was the one who took me in when I was out of work"

Olan Chapman worked for a major electronics firm when the layoff order came down from upstairs. The nation reeled from a stock market crash. Down sizing became a household word. America stayed home as gas prices soared, and television sales dwindled to an all time low. Olan's first reaction to the pink slip was disbelief. Then he stopped by the local tap room to tie one on, and lady luck chose to smile on this Phi bet ta kappa with no children and two pet rabbits. He had no sooner found a sympathetic bar stool, when an ex school mate named Marty Simmons sauntered in. Marty was a fellow computer geek and knew everybody who was anybody in Lower Elk County, New Jersey.

"Talk about some good timing," said Olan Chapman, "Marty knew Harold, and Marty's wife Lori came up with this house in Hobbs Creek."

"I hate it here," said Ivy Chapman who grew up with tar and cement, and barely squeaked through a South Philly high school, "And if Lori doesn't stop shoving her tits in your face, I'll shove a broomstick up her real estate."

"Lori's just tall that's all," said Chapman with a small cough, "I thought you two were chummy."

"She goes to the gym for exercise," said Ivy dryly, "I rake leaves while you sit in an air conditioned office."

The Chapmans first met at an Orange County bar in Kissimmee, Florida. They were in the Orlando area to visit Walt Disney's Animal Kingdom. The year was 2004. Six named hurricanes blew through the Sunshine State in less than three months. Floridians were frightened. You could see the apprehension in taunt faces at food markets, gas stations, supply centers where home owners flocked to buy bottled water and plywood. News media suggested that the Sunshine State be renamed the hurricane state. One isolated email wanted to move Florida north to Alaska.

Hurricane Charlie was the second blow of that busy season. Charlie came ashore at Punta Gorda, raged through Zolfo Springs and stormed through Orange County before moving north. Winds clocked between 110 and 150 mph. State damages reached 13 billion, plus. Charlie also spawned sudden tornadoes, closed down Disney's Animal Kingdom, and put Olan Chapman on a bar stool next to Ivy Ann Goya.

"I've never met a girl who would sit at a bar and drink carrot juice," said the thirty year old computer programmer.

"It's an ice breaker,"   replied the dark eyed woman with a belly button ring and too many credit cards,   "I tried the *drop the hanky gimmick*, but the only person who picked it up was a girl."

They got married in a fever hotter than a Jalepeno pepper. They designated Hurricane Charlie as their best man, and set up housekeeping in a Buffalo City condo near where Olan worked. Two pay raises later, they bought a split level in Hyde Park, not far from Niagara Falls. Now, seven years later, they were in a log cabin not far off the South Jersey Pine Barrens. Money light. Mortgage heavy. Still childless. Meanwhile, the two rabbits multiplied to twenty-two. Olan was dis enchanted with Ivy's hairy arms and loose spending habits. Ivy was fed up with Olan's drinking and weird ways, including several suicide attempts.

"I'm not suicidal,"   said Olan Chapman.

"Olan, you're suicidal."

"Am not."

"Are, too."

"Am not."

"Olan, let's review your track record,"   said Ivy, "The insurance building downtown caught fire. You climbed to the roof. The fire company had to save you while they put out the fire. One fire man carried you down. A second fire fighter brought down your whiskey bottle."

"I was a bit depressed that night,"   admitted husband Olan.

"Let's talk about the Cedar Bridge incident," said Ivy Chapman.

"I'd rather not."

"Olan, the freaking bridge is only ten foot off the water," said wife Ivy,   "All you did was fracture a toe. . . and what about your Niagara Falls episode in a barrel?"

"That was not a suicide attempt,"   said husband Olan,   "I was on a crusade for a worth while cause."

"Olan, nobody goes over Horseshoe Falls to raise public awareness of male dysfunctional disorder."

Maybe it was rabbit fever, or the perfect moon hoving over the woodsy back road. Maybe it was the lusty image of Harold Stottermeyer pumping off his twenty-one year old secretary. But, somehow Olan Chapman's right hand picked that precarious moment to to creep up his wife's skirt.

"Olan!"

"I don't know why you're on a diet any way," said Olan Chapman in a voice growing sloppier by the moment,   "I like fat thighs."

"Olan, keep your freaking hands on the wheel !" cried Ivy, "It's bad enough you are suicidal. I can not take sex and suicide at the same time."

"I'm not suicidal."

"Olan, anyone who puts a forty five to their head is suicidal."

"I am not suicidal !" cried Olan Chapman, "I just wanted to show the world why it's dangerous to keep a gun in the house."

"Olan, that's bullshit," replied Ivy, "The next chamber held the shell. If I had not showed up when I did. . well. . your brains would have been blown all over Hyde Park."

"I   AM   NOT   SUICIDAL!"   yelled Olan Chapman, briefly taking eyes off the road to glare at his wife.

Moments later, the Chapmans' silver van broke through the wood guard rail at Dead Man's Curve. It bounced down the steep gravel incline, and crashed into a hefty scrub oak.

Screams filled the night air.

The next car around the bend, pulled over and dialed 911.

CHAPTER 2

Fifty odd years gone by changes most things. Even Hobbs Creek. Jim Bob's Hardware is gone. Likewise, Marty Corson's Fuel Oil Business. Millie's Market surrendered to a giant shopping mall. The fire department is no longer volunteer. The old clapboard station house at Elm and Main is now a steel structure, clothed with glass and brick veneer,

Also, there's Barney Kibble's taxi service that died when his mud caked, station wagon blew a motor rod sometime in the mid sixties. No one's sure what became of Barney – or his hearing aids – or the bumper sticker that read *I Like Ike.* Tri County Taxi replaced the one man operation with a slew of cabs that actually make an effort to observe traffic laws.

And, Old Man Mayo's Esso is now an Exxon Mobil Station with today's *sticker shock* prices that mark a sign of the times. The soda machine that would some times spit your coin back with the drink, now takes dollar bills.

Somethings never change.

Namely, Jeeter Potts.

"Isabel, where is he?" asked Police Chief, Adam Quayle while covering the mouth piece to the duty phone.

"Home, Sir," replied a crisp voice from the dispatch desk in the next room.

"He's not home and he's not answering his cell," said Quayle who had County General Hospital on one line, while trying to raise Jeeter Potts on a second line.

"Then, he's probably at Fishers Pond."

Adam Quayle brushed smooth a pesky shirt wrinkle and rose to stare out the plate glass window that normally overlooked a dozen black and whites. Some on duty, some not. Today was different. All units were out but two. Black Friday was over. Good tiding sounds filled the festive air. And with the Christmas spirit, came overtime pay for the Hobbs Creek police force.

Quayle poured some black coffee and flopped into the squeaky swivel chair that came with the territory. He frowned. Justifying the holiday budget to Mayor Willard Green III also came with the territory. He rose from the desk and returned to the window.

"Fishers Pond?" he queried turning his good ear toward the open door that separated dispatch from

QUANTUM ROOTS

Quayle's inner office.

"Fishers Pond, Sir,"   came the reply.

Adam Quayle became top cop in 1977 at former Chief William Brennan's retirement party. Quayle was now over retirement age, himself. His hair was gone, teeth capped. His somber green eyes watched a homeless dog cross the empty lot, and head toward a street corner Santa with a deep voice and itchy beard. Said Quayle, "I hope Jeeter knows we have everybody out covering the parade."

"I doubt if Jeeter knows what day it is, Suh."

Jeeter Potts was another working relic. The frail sergeant also qualified to be the world's oldest jitter bug. He had Adam Quayle's vote to be sure. Pott's career as station clerk spanned five decades. He was on his third wife and served as pop pop to a dozen rug rats. He wore giant earphones for music, and drove a gas hungry antique tag.

Jeeter's latest wedding woes came when his current wife Teena got a butterfly tattoed on her back side. Teena pointed out that a tattoo was no longer a guy thing. Jeeter replied that if he wanted someone with a tattoo, he would have married a sailor. Or maybe a truck driver. Teena then locked the bedroom door, and Jeeter was now back to tossing stones at Fishers

Pond.

"So that leaves us to hold down the fort," said Adam Quayle peering over eye glasses toward the door that opened to dispatch, "I don't suppose you would be up to running an errand."

"Not me, Suh," replied Isabel Jackson, "You could not pay me enough to brave that mess. No suh. Just look out your window. You can't tell the shoppers from the paraders."

"Thank you, Isabel."

"You are welcome, and Suh?"

"Yes, Isabel?"

"Don't let the door hit you in the ass."

"Thank you, Isabel."

"You are welcome, Suh."

Adam Quayle strapped on a stubborn seat belt and switched on the bubblegum light to get onto Main Street. Crowds moved aside like cattle. Some gave ground politely. Others cursed and made middle finger motions. Quayle quietly raised the driver's window and headed northeast.

The road from Hobbs Creek to Lake Powhatan cuts across Route 91, runs another two miles north, and dead ends into the resort gates. The entire trek takes place within a twelve-square mile area charted off as

QUANTUM ROOTS

Hobbs Creek Township.

An earthy metamorphose takes place during the short journey. Swamp cedars give way to oaks and scrub pines. Cattail sprouts change to thorny stalks. Mud to moss. Fishing takes backseat to hunting, and a distant howl can often give a tender foot the jitters. Adam Quayle paused to greet the gate guard, awash in flood lights.

"Good to see you, Henry," said Quayle.

"They are calling for lots more snow in the morning," said the guard pushing a button to open two wrought iron gates, "Better be getting the long johns out of moth balls."

"Thank you, Henry."

"And Sir?"

"Yes, Henry."

"Your right headlight's out."

"Thank you, Henry."

Cabins surround Lake Powhatan like a wagon train. Most of the single story dwellings have a front porch, a tool shed outback and no garage. Some have heat and air. Others serve as a second home for those who would escape the monotony of daily work loads and pokey stop lights.

Most folks love the park grounds which are an oasis of nature. The cedar lake sparkles like cut glass under bright skies. Oak trees flutter with robins come spring. Squirrels rob seed from handy bird feeders, while a bold mallard might peck at your screen door for stale breadcrumbs.

"I hate it here," said Ivy Chapman replying to Adam Quayle's door rap at Cabin Eighteen.

"It's often hard for city folk to adjust in the pines," replied Quayle, "Did you ever get those allergy pills that Doc Belvins recommended?"

"Tried them the first year we were here," said Ivy Chapman, "They work good except in the spring."

Through July and August, this rustic retreat bustles with lazy fishermen and fast boats. Swim suits hang from droopy clotheslines. Card players gather under the lakeside pavilion. And twice monthly, the VFW still drums up a square dance. Then by October, the happy waters return to dormacy, as do the island beaches a few miles to the southeast.

"And I hate salty water and sticky sand," said Ivy Chapman, "Is Olan okay or is this more questions about the accident?"

"You didn't seem to be answering your phone," said Adam Quayle by way of explanation.

QUANTUM ROOTS

"I was out back feeding rabbits and hanging up wash," said Ivy Chapman, "Dryer's busted, wouldn't you know. It's that sales lady with the big tits that got us moved in here. Olan loves rum and big tits. She could move Olan into a tent if she went bra-less and showed up with a bottle."

A flushing Adam Quayle used a request for water to check out the kitchen. After which, he visited the bathroom as a ruse to peek under the bed and paw through a clothes closet.

At one time, Adam Quayle was the most sought after bachelor in Lower Elk County. His wavy blond hair and crisp green eyes served to flood a busy event calendar. Somehow, that special one never came along. Now, decades later, his main agenda was playing pinocle with town council, and eating late dinner at Chappys Cafe - formally Edna's. Ironically, Quayle was halfway through a roast beef sandwich at Chappy's, when Olan Chapman - no relation - crashed into the scrub oak.

"Good thing you had your seat belt on," called out Quayle from a back bedroom, "Shame Olan didn't have his on....and his hands on the wheel."

"Olan had his hands up my crotch," said Ivy Chapman.

"Yes, it said that in the report."

"I told him to go play with himself."

"Yes, it also said that in the report,"

"And if he got tired," said Ivy Chapman, "I told him to switch hands."

"He does play a good hand of pinocle," said Quayle sliding away from the topic.

"It's nice he has friends," said Ivy.

"You are welcome to join the wives," said Adam Quayle, "They could use one more card player, not to mention another hostess."

"I'm not very good at bridge," said Ivy, "And since we are friends, I won't ask you for your search warrant."

"I'm not searching," said Adam Quayle, "Just looking."

When the first of two ambulances reached the crash site that party night, the three man EMS squad found Ivy Chapman in shock, and Olan Chapman in a coma. The responding fire truck returned to Carson City. The Chapmans were transported to County General. Quayle became involved because Dead Man's Curve lies just inside Hobbs Creek Township. Later, Ivy was released, and Olan retained for observation.

"All I've been doing is carting off to the hospital and back," said Ivy Chapman. A moment later she added, "I hope the little twerp wakes up before I run out of cab fare. . . I have half a mind to box his ears . .. I suppose he will get a ticket for reckless driving."

"Was Olan drinking?" asked Quayle.

"Of course," replied Ivy Chapman, "We came from a party."

"How drunk was he?" asked Quayle.

"Plastered," said Ivy Chapman.

Chief Adam Quayle first met Olan Chapman at the intersection of Elm and Main Streets. Quayle had just turned to pull into police headquarters when Chapman ran the red light and broadsided the squad car. Quayle was sober. Chapman checked out to be under the influence.

"He looked at the firehouse across the street and told me he was a firefighter," said Quayle, "We slapped him in the holding tank to wait arraignment. That's where Jeeter Potts discovered your husband was a cracker jack card player."

Olan Chapman was a crackerjack pinocle player. He knew the bids. He knew the play. He could run two suits out before the opposition could pull a trick, and that earned him the nick name of *Slam.*. Together, Potts and Chapman won the firehouse championship three years running.

"Well, you caught a real break with this latest accident," said Quayle to Ivy Chapman, "The hospital never took an alcohol reading."

"Thank God for small favors," said Ivy.

"We have a variety of social service programs here in Lower Elks County," said Quayle, "You might find that of some help."

"Thank you Adam," said Ivy, "I'm afraid that won't work for Olan. He's not really an alcoholic. He just likes to drink."

The graying police chief stood at the giant picture window in the front room. The cabin had been put in backwards. The living room over looked the water. The bedrooms faced the road. Quayle's mild green eyes panned the frozen lake. He said, "Those kids should not be out there without supervision."

"That's the Grundy twins next door," said Ivy, "They got new ice skates for Christmas."

"We opened our gifts on Christmas Day," said Adam Quayle who was one of five siblings.

"They are allowed to open one gift early," explained Ivy Chapman, "Somehow they picked the box that held the ice skates."

"Is Olan really suicidal?" asked Adam Quayle watching one twin throw a snowball at the other twin who ran off screaming.

"You have been talking to Jeeter ," said Ivy.

"Jeeter and Olan seem to hit it off," said the Hobbs Creek Police Chief, "Jeeter also swears he knows Chapman from a long time back."

"Has Jeeter ever been to New York?"

"Jeeter Potts has never been out of the Pine Barrens," said Adam Quayle.

Ivy Chapman couldn't help but smile. She turned back to the window as the Grundy twins trudged up from the lake. Their mother, Maryann Grundy would be back shortly. Ivy pulled the lace curtain closed and spun on a heel to face Quayle. She said, "I've had Olan's stomach pumped out twice since we've lived here."

"Sleeping pills?" asked Quayle.

"Valium," said Ivy, "Also known as Antenex or Diazepam. Doctor prescribed. Olan suffers from hypertension, anxiety, insomnia."

"I didn't know," said Adam Quayle.

"We don't let that go public," said Ivy, "Back in Niagara County, Olan tried to go over the Falls in a row boat. Two EMS guys with a chopper and a grappling hook saved his bacon."

Somehow, the pilot got the craft into position behind Olan's boat. The second man tossed the rope. Head winds made the going tough. After a half dozen tries, the grappling hook finally caught under the stern seat, just as the bow reached the top of the falls. After which, the pilot dragged the boat backward to safety. The headline grabber was the first of three efforts by Olan Chapman to go over the Falls. Two other attempts failed because of inclement weather.

"Olan's a rainbow of moods," said Ivy Chap man, "Including hostility. Fortunately, I can beat the shit out of him, but it doesn't solve anything. He goes right back to drinking and up pops the devil."

"Has Olan ever suffered from amnesia?" asked Adam Quayle.

"No."

"Maybe a concussion from football days?"

"Olan never played football."

"Any family history of dementia." asked Quayle.

"I wouldn't know," replied Ivy.

"Does Olan ever walk in his sleep?" asked Quayle.

Suddenly, Ivy Chapman's face stiffened. She turned from the window to face Quayle eyeball to eyeball as she asked, "What's happened, Adam? . .

.why are you really here?"

"The hospital desk has been trying to call you all morning," said Police Chief, Adam Quayle shifting feet uncomfortably. Then his voice softened as he said, "Olan Chapman has gone missing."

CHAPTER 3

Two weeks before Christmas, a new vagrant ordinance prompted Corky Tabor III to move his *Work For Food* sign from Hobbs Creek to Mt Loyal City. At a stormy Thursday night meeting, Hobbs Creek town council voted 3 to 2 to ban all panhandlers from Hobbs Creek street corners. Township Mayor, Willard Green III gained strong voter approval when he broke the 2 to2 deadlock.

Motorists cheered.

Opposition booed.

Shoppers gave the third generation mayor a standing ovation, while panhandlers everywhere stole the media limelight with that timeless holiday outburst, *bah hum bug.*

Light snow fell as Corky Tabor III stepped from the bus onto a back street of the Lower Elk County seat. He paused to adjust a lumpy brown sack and thank the driver for a freebie.

"This is not the neighborhood for a white boy," said the black bus driver.

"We're no longer welcome in Hobbs Creek" said Corky speaking for township's 250 homeless, "City fathers got that new ordinance through. They claim we're disturbing the motorists and upsetting traffic patterns."

"Try Carson City," suggested the driver.

"I have friends here," said Corky.

"Of course you do."

Corky Tabor III was the grandson of Charlton Corky Tabor who was Hobbs Creek's first ever panhandler. Corky Charlton Tabor also owned bragging rights as a witness to super human feats, executed by previous Hobbs Creek Police Chief, William Bo Brennan, who was the strongest man in Lower Elk County. Tales of Brennan's strength range from a fishy odor to sheer flap doodle.

It's said Brennan once rolled a getaway car upside down with his bare hands, then used a jack handle to cuff the holdup man to a doorpost. In another incident, he tossed an entire motorcycle gang out of Binkys Liquor Store with no call for back up. And it was Corky Tabor who saw Brennan hand brace a broken timber under the Cedar Gap Bridge while a runaway freight train crossed to safe ground.

Pure or colored, Charlton Tabor passed these tales on to Corky III, who's schoolyard ambition was to write a great American novel entitled Hobbs Creek.

Eventually, Charlton's grandson became a connoisseur of wines, whiskey and cough syrup. Thus, he never succeeded with the fine art of story telling. Instead, he wound up walking the homeless alleys of Hobbs Creek until the recent holiday ordinance moved him on.

Merry Christmas.

There was a Corky II, who graduated from Harvard and opened a law practice. He was eventually ousted from the Tabor family due to incompatibility issues.

Streetlights flickered on as some stores closed early despite yule time shoppers. Iron gates sealed off windows. Double padlocks secured doors. Corky paused to watch a model train display, reminiscent of days when Corky's biggest battles were curfews and report cards. Times were happy then, money loose. Corky's parents held grand expectations that their lone child would someday become a doctor, or lawyer, or maybe even the President Of The United States. Then, Corky II ran off with a neighbor's wife, and Corky III went from a city penthouse to the Jersey Pine Barrens to live with his grandfather.

Suddenly, a window curtain closed on the model railroad show, and the current Corky Tabor moved on.

More stores closed.

QUANTUM ROOTS

More lights went out.

Corky found an alley with a dumpster before setting up squatters rights. Dumpsters can be a god send to street people. Along with food scraps, these giant waste cans sometimes offer cast off clothing and shelter against howling winds. It is wise to listen for approaching trash trucks.

This particular dumpster coughed up half a banana and two cigarettes. Corky was halfway through the second cigarette when a voice came from a dark stairwell.

"Hey ! And what do we have here?"

Corky heard the voice before he saw the gangly figure sprint up the concrete steps. Instinctively, Corky wrapped up his meager belongings and tucked the canvass pack under an arm. He glanced quickly to the alley opening and back. Warning bells gripped his stomach. He looked like the proverbial frightened deer caught in vehicle headlights.

"I think we got ourselves a whitey," cackled a second boyish voice bouncing up the stairwell from the row house basement.

"We got a white boy up here !" yelled a third youth emerging into view.

"Looks like stomp bait to me," said a fourth voice too deep to be a teenager.

Main Street lay a good hundred feet to Corky's rear, Trash cans and closed doors loomed ahead. Neither choice would become a workable option. As Corky Tabor turned to run, three more gang members blocked any hope to escape.

"You are on our turf," said a black youth with orange hair. He waved a 38 caliber gun as he bragged, "This used to belong to a cop that invaded our turf. Now it belongs to me."

Corky's mouth opened but his voice failed.

"You know who we are?" asked a Latino with a gold tooth and a foot long machete.

Corky shuddered. His head wag said no.

"We are the Black Dragons and you're on our ground," whispered an Oriental with a burr hair cut, "Nobody invades our territory, not even the cops. What's in the back pack?"

"I carry a knife," said Corky his finding voice, "But you can have it. I don't want any trouble."

"You don't want any trouble?"

"I don't want any trouble," whimpered Corky.

"He doesn't want any trouble," mimicked the Latino as he kissed the cold steel machete.

QUANTUM ROOTS

The Oriental laughed and shoved Corky III over a discarded milk crate and onto the icy pavement. All six boys then formed a circle around their helpless victim. The black youth with orange hair pulled the 38 special. He pointed the loaded gun at Corky's head.

Corky began to sob.

"Wait," ordered the Oriental, "There are many eyes watching from behind closed shades. This is our chance to send the neighborhood a message to stay off our turf. This is our chance to send the world a message. We will let these prying eyes watch us stomp this piece of shit into a blot on the sidewalk. Then, even the Black Hawks will fear to invade our territory !"

Corky curled into a fetal postion as the brutal beating began. The boys took turns kicking head and rib areas. Screams filled the night air. Window blinds opened and closed. No one called 911.

Eventually, the screams stopped.

The stomping went on.

Seconds turned to minutes.

Minutes that dragged on.

The Latino with the gold tooth was first to notice. He nudged the black youth who motioned to the Oriental to check the alley opening.

The kicking stopped.

Corky lay still.

Blood trickled from all head cavities.

"And who the hell are you?" demanded the Oriental looking toward Main Street.

The man who filled the alley entrance way was little more than a silhouette. He stood with legs apart, head erect, arms at sides. He wore a flat brim hat, drab clothes. A streetlight highlighted his tiny mustache and stolid eyes. A silver star shone off a baggy cowboy vest.

"This is Dragon turf," yelled the Oriental, "Move on or die !"

No reply.

"He's packing," whispered one gang member who noticed a lazy pistol that hung from a break-away holster.

"Kill him !" ordered the Oriental.

The black youth handed the thirty-eight to the Latino and cried, "Shoot him !"

The Latino shoved the firearm back at the black boy and cried, "You shoot him !"

Another long moment passed as the black youth fumbled with the safety. Cursing, the Oriental grabbed the revolver and whirled to face the ominous silhouette framed in the alleyway entrance.

"Okay sucka," cried the Oriental, "You die !"

The Colt 45 appeared to jump into the new comer's hand. He shot from the left hip. He appeared to fan the weapon with his right hand. Five shots rang out as a single sound. The first bullet caught the Oriental between the eyes. After which, four more boys stiffened and fell to the pavement.

The silhouette paused to reload.

The sixth boy ducked into a stairwell that led to a neighborhood safe house. The solid wood door was now bolted. The boy screamed for help and remounted the concrete steps.

The Black Dragon den hid at the far end of the alley. The boy's row home sat halfway down the block. He stepped over bleeding bodies and took off running. Waves of panic gripped his gut. Cold terror filled the eyes of this fourteen year old. His screams parted closed curtains and brought his robust mama into the alleyway.

The silhouette finished reloading.

"Alfie," screamed the woman,, "You git yo black ass in this house right now !"

The silhouette aimed the weapon and fired. The cartridge caught the boy on the dead run. The hollow point shell made a small hole in the back of the head.

The bullet took off the boy's face, coming out.

CHAPTER 4

FIC Headquarters: Warrenton, Virginia

Jeremy Wade parked his motor scooter in front of the Federal Intelligence Center, just off the Eastern By Pass. He removed a bicycle helmet, and smacked down a springy hair cowlick as he hobbled up the concrete steps. A heavy cast wrapped the special agent's right foot. His ID badge was missing.

"I need to see it," said the stony faced guard at the entrance door.

"For chris'sake, Stanley," cried the junior agent with the dimpled grin, "You have a metal detector, a bomb sensor, a scanner that can steal the numbers off my credit card. Not to mention, you damn well know who I am."

"I need to see the badge," insisted the guard.

"He needs to see your ID," said a senior officer on his way out.

Jeremy Wade brushed aside a red tie and checked an inside suit pocket. He slapped trouser pockets and opened a wallet over stocked with credit cards. He found the required photo ID in a rear pocket, and clipped it to his belt.

"It's supposed to be visible," called the guard over a disappearing shoulder.

Jeremy ignored the comment and entered a revolving door in time to meet a man with a cast on his left foot. The two casts collided head on. The two men yelped.

"I think you are going the wrong way," said Jeremy Wade clutching his right foot.

"Damn," said Martin Swan clutching his left foot, "I never get this direction thing right."

"Martin Swan!" cried the junior agent, "Holy cow, you're not the Martin Swan with the Invisible Six?"

"The same," admitted the slender agent with the bow tie and knobby knees, "And this is my wife, Jodie."

"Martin Swan!" exclaimed Jeremy trying not to stare down the girl's blouse, "You're almost legendary, Sir. And tales of the Invisible Six. Wow! Definitely movie fodder."

Martin Swan and The Invisible Six escapades encircle the globe: blowing up bridges in the face of the Taliban; trading gunfire with Colombian drug lords; rescuing kidnapped maidens.

QUANTUM ROOTS

Said Jeremy Wade, "My favorite saga was the Thanksgiving Day gunfight at Black Water Crossing."

The story goes that Cuban-assisted terrorists tried to smuggle an explosive threat into Washington DC. The plan was to truck the cargo from Florida into Virginia. The bad guys would utilize the Suwanee River, a network of back roads and a bridge encoded Black Water Crossing. Luckily, details reached Swan and The Invisible Six in time to thwart the impending disaster.

"Well done I must say, Sir," said Jeremy Wade with a low whistle.

"Thank you, agent."

"The explosive cargo turned out to be fire crackers hidden in pumpkins," scoffed Jodie trying to light a cigarette inside the revolving door.

"It was not fireworks," corrected Martin Swan, "They were hand grenades and some of our vital bureaucrats could have been injured. Also, that wasn't the interior plot behind Black Water Crossing. The real threat went even deeper than that."

"Of course that's classified," said Martin's wife Jodie who was omitted from all briefings.

"And remains classified for national security reasons," said Martin Swan.

"Of course," coughed Jeremy Wade while dodging Jodie's cigarette smoke.

A fat man with stocky arms entered the far side of the revolving door. The unknown intruder had slipped by Stanley, only to be turned back at a second check point, which opened to a main hall that led to department check points. The stocky intruder was now back in the revolving door, rejected and angry. He grabbed the hand bar and shoved so hard that neither Wade nor the Swans could make an exit.

"Yo !" screamed Jodie.

"Welcome to headquarters merry-go-round," said Jeremy hopping on one foot to keep pace with the revolving door, now picking up speed.

"So how did you wind up in that cast?" asked Swan of Wade.

"Karate kicking," replied Jeremy, who really injured his foot stepping into a pothole, "I missed the bad guy and connected with a steel light post. . . and you?"

"My stepson hit me with a hammer," said Swan, "I think the kid hates me."

"Martin !" cried Jodie Fields Santinio Swan, "Timmy does not hate you. He was trying to catch a water bug and what the hell does this fat guy think he's doing !"

The unknown intruder now held the hand bar at arm's reach, and drove with pumping legs like a fullback plowing up center. The revolving door continued to pick up speed. Martin Swan grabbed the hand bar on his side of the door. Jeremy Wade fell into Jodie. Cried Swan, "Agent, are you feeling up my wife !"

"Sir, I'm not feeling up anybody."

"Agent, you've got my wife by the tits !"

"Sir," cried Jeremy Wade, "I'm just trying to hold on to something."

As the revolving door opened to the lobby, Jodie ducked out and re entered the partition that held the unknown intruder. Quickly, she removed a black jack concealed in her giant handbag. When the opening approached the outside, she cold cocked the deranged being who fell into security's waiting grasp.

"Good job, Mrs Swan," said the bleak faced guard as he summoned back-up.

"C'mon Martin," said Jodie Swan grabbing her weaving mate by a coat sleeve, "You promised me Paris and I'm holding you to it."

The Department For Paranormal Activities sits on the second floor of the FIC building. Jeremy gave Jodie a wistful parting look and summoned the elevator. He straightened his tie as he entered the DPA office.

"You are late," said Lieutenant General, Alexis Grumman.

"I got caught in traffic," explained Jeremy.

"That's bullshit agent," said the slender woman as she popped a peppermint candy and sipped ice water, "Motor scooters don't get caught in traffic. . .I see you have met the Swans."

Jeremy Wade surveyed a operations room loaded with scanners, computers and one gigantic wall screen. Corner monitors displayed all building and parking lot activity. Said Jeremy, "The night has a thousand eyes."

"It better," replied the DPA director.

"The Swans are leaving for a honeymoon?" said Jeremy in questioning tones.

"The Invisible Six are dismantled," said the slender woman as an explanation, "Martin Swan is now retired."

"How will that impact national security?" asked Jeremy.

"I'm sure we'll survive," said Alexis.

"She looks like his daughter," said Jeremy.

"Pocket your fantasies, agent."

"Yes Ma'am."

QUANTUM ROOTS

Alexis Grumman was among the first United States women to earn the rank of Lieutenant General in the armed forces. The three star, single mother served tours in Korea, Germany and Vietnam. She wore the Legion Of Merit, and two Meritorious Service medals on her smart uniform jacket. She served much of her military career coordinating intelligence with remote field operations.

"So, here I am having meaningful talks with people who witness UFO's and believe in river monsters," said Alexis with a hollow laugh. She gave Jeremy a finger motion that meant wait. She tapped an intercom and told someone named Doug that *net working* was down again. Her brown eyes looked back at Jeremy as she said, "One of our *servers* isn't working."

"Doug, I presume," said Jeremy.

Alexis smiled saying, "I see you are not into computers. Our servers feed network data."

"I work mostly outside, Ma'am."

"Do you know why you are here?"

"I was told it had something to do with the Helena Hollister case," said the junior agent, "I did work that assignment."

Helena Hollister was a Big Apple cocktail waitress who grabbed the family fortune by framing husband Rodney with murder. She had legal help from moonstruck attorney, Justin Pierce. She enlisted lethal help from a Hobbs Creek handyman named Abel Johnson, who perished in a cabin fire. Eventually, Helena and Justin slipped away with the money, as two backwoods lawmen failed to unravel the mystery of who killed Elmer Kane. The case went unsolved from 1958 until after 911 when Helena Hollister surfaced in Right Bank, Paris.

"I understand you uncovered Helena Hollister living as Anna Ward.," said Alexis while studying the facts sheet.

"I had some help from Interpol," replied the junior agent, "I worked out of T.A.G. (Tracking Agency Global) back then."

"Who is William Brennan?" asked Alexis.

"Brennan and Emmet Walker Thomas first investigated the Elmer Kane homicide," said Jeremy, "Brennan was Hobbs Creek's police chief in 1958. Lieutenant Thomas worked out of Mt Loyal, which is the Lower Elk County seat."

"And Adam Quayle?" asked Alexis.

QUANTUM ROOTS

"Quayle is the current police chief for Hobbs Creek," said Jeremy, "He was my stateside contact in chasing down Helena Hollister and Justin Pierce."

Alexis jumped from her desk upon hearing that *net working* was back up. She grabbed a pointer and faced the big screen. She called for *Clip One* and asked Jeremy Wade, "Who is Jesse Joe Jacks?"

"That, I don't know," replied Jeremy.

"These film clips are a bit graphic," said Alexis.

"Yes, Ma'am."

"Have you been briefed on this vigilante?"

"No Ma'am."

Clip One took place in a Mount Loyal City convenience store. A hooded bandit robbed the lone cashier and turned to face an unannounced obstacle. A vigilante blocked the exit door. The bandit grabbed a nearby hostage, and pointed a gun to her ear. The vigilante shot the gun out of the man's hand. The woman screamed as the shell passed by her head, then fainted to the floor.

Cursing, the bandit retaliated with some cans from a food display. The vigilante picked the cans off in mid air, then put the final bullet between the eye holes in the bandit's hood.

Jeremy Wade grimaced.

"You okay?"   asked Alexis.

"I guess he doesn't take prisoners,"   said Jeremy.

"Doug," called out Alexis, "Roll the next clip."

Clip Two took place in a remote Carson City parking lot. Four boys followed two female shoppers from a curbside retail store. The two women were behind the building before they heard trailing foot steps. They quickened the pace. The footsteps grew louder. The women dropped their packages and ran for the car. As they locked the doors, panting boys surrounded their vehicle. Protruding tongues licked at the windows. Dirty noses pressed against the safety glass.

The driver fumbled through a messy hand bag for car keys. She just found the ignition slot when an ax head smashed through the wind shield.

The two women screamed.

A second ax blade cut through the rear window .

More screams.

"Doug, pause it there,"   called out Alexis. Turning to Jeremy she said, "Watch this next portion, closely."

Fours quick shots rang out as the video clip continued. Four boys lurched and fell to the lumpy macadam, one on each side of the car. Jeremy faintly moved his head in disbelief. Awe painted his mellow features as he asked, "How did a shell hit the boy standing behind the trunk?"

Alexis rolled back the video clip. She pointed to a dark area on the screen and said, "Our vigilante stands here in the shadows. He's out of the security camera's range, but within shooting distance. His first shot takes down the boy standing on the hood. Bullets two and three take down the boys on each side of the car. Bullet four goes through this ax hole in the wind shield, between the two women, and out a rear hole to hit the fourth gang member."

"Incredible," whispered Jeremy Wade.

"Unbelievable for sure," agreed the video technician as he transferred computer data to a giant air cooled projector, "And it's not tricked-out security film. I did the dubbing, myself."

Alexis set the pointer on a black computer desk and reached for a water glass. She munched on an ice cube as the last video clip played. Jeremy waved off an offer of candy mints, and watched while three armed youths closed in on a vagrant, wrapped by an Indian blanket. The vagrant sat yogi style, up a blind alley not far from where the vigilante's first shooting took place. As the gang members drew near, the vagrant shot through the blanket, killing all three instantly.

"This our best picture of this vigilante," said Alexis picking up the pointer, "We get a good shot of his face and revolver as he sheds the blanket. Our weapons expert figures the gun as a Colt 45. Probably made in the mid-fifties, judging by barrel length and handle wear. The bullets are hollow point according to the medical examiner. They make a tiny hole going in, and a big hole coming out."

"This vigilante is not a nice person," said the junior agent, "Do we have a positive ID?"

"We have three," replied Alexis, "William Brennan, Charlton Tabor Sr and Adam Quayle positively identify this man as Jesse Joe Jacks ."

"And it's my mission to bring him in?" asked Jeremy Wade.

"It's your mission to verify the ID," said Alexis , "We will let local authorities apprehend this man."

Jeremy Wade paused by the door.

"You have a question?" asked Alexis.

"Yes, Ma'am."

"I thought you might," said Alexis.

"This vigilante has not crossed any state lines," said Jeremy Wade, "He's certainly not an unidentified flying object. He's not a river monster. So, why is this case in the Department Of Paranormal Activities?"

QUANTUM ROOTS

Lt General Alexis Grumman put a phone call on hold. She sipped more ice water, slipped another candy mint between her nudish lips and picked up a grainy photo fax. She turned back to the junior agent and flatly said, "Jeremy. . . . Jesse Joe Jacks died fifty years ago."

"Oh."

"Yes, oh."

"Well, everybody has a twin," said Jeremy Wade, "Or so they so. Actually, my father was a twin, and so was my Uncle Louis. Only the twin to my Uncle Louis was a female they named Louella. Consequently, I wound up with an Uncle Lou and an Aunt Lou ."

"Fascinating," replied Alexis Grumman, dryly. Then after some thought she said, "We might have a twin here, Jeremy."

"You're not convinced."

"I'll tell you what bothers me," said Alexis pointing at split screen photographs on a wall monitor, "Look at the garb. Here's a grainy picture of Jesse Joe Jacks, sent here from Hobbs Creek dispatch. The picture is dated 1958. Jacks is wearing a black hat, red scarf, tattered ammo vest and a left handed holster. Now, study the picture on the right. This video of the vigilante was taken two days ago. Both men have on the same clothes."

Silence.

"How does this happen?"   asked Alexis,

More silence.

"I'm not into science fiction," continued the female Lieutenant General, "And. . . I don't believe in super natural. There has to be a plausible explanation for this."

"Yes Ma'am."

"Find it."

"Yes Ma'am."

"And Jeremy. . .

"Yes Ma'am?"

"Scrap the motorbike and sign out a car."

"Ma'am, I do have a cast on my foot."

"Jeremy, don't bullshit me," replied Alexis Grumman, "Your foot's not broken, and your cycle riding skills leave something to be desired. We're still paying damages for two motor bikes, and a pedestrian you ran over outside that bull fighting ring in Spain."

"Yes, Ma'am."

CHAPTER 5

Time heals all wounds, or so the adage goes.

Sometimes, tragedy heals wounds.

The Tabor clan had not held a family assembly since Attorney Charlton Corky Jr passed his bar exam - while Charlton Corky Sr passed out on a bar stool. Matters worsened down the road when Charlton "Corky The Third" moved in with Pop Pop, who taught the boy how to raid a food dumpster and sleep on a park bench. After that, everybody stopped talking to every body.

Change happens.

The stomping death of Corky III now melted icy barriers, and reunited the Tabor family at Lower Elk County Cemetery. Father and son stood side by side near a tombstone that read R.I.P. Ellie Tabor, who was Charlton Sr's wife of three years. Ellie died giving birth to Charlton Jr. Some say it was that tragic event that sent the elder Tabor off on the road to nowhere.

Aunt Rose and Uncle Bill were in attendance with the twins who were busy hurling snowballs at grave markers. Cousin Roberta stood quietly, constraining a squirmy cat at the end of a frozen leash. Local friends also looked on. Jeeter Potts received a stiff warning to shut down a transistor radio, leftover from yesteryear. Police Chief, Adam Quayle arrived wiith Special Agent, Jeremy Wade. The two lawmen reunited at the Hobbs Creek Station House, and were here now to question Corky Tabor Sr.

"This is not a good time for sure," apologized Jeremy as the minister said *dearly beloved,* "But Tabor has no phone number or address."

"Wait here at curbside, Jeremy," said Adam Quayle, "I'll bring Corky over after the service."

Time passed.

The sermon ended.

The last yellow rose dropped into the casket.

Adam Quayle returned with the elder Corky Tabor in tow, as icy snow fell and winds picked up. Said Corky while eying Wade's ID, "Don't know what I can tell you that you don't already know."

"You can tell me how Jesse Joe Jacks died," said the special agent.

"I was there!" cried Corky.

"Yes, I know," said Jeremy.

"Happened right in Pykes Pit," said the Hobbs Creek pan handler, "Worse electrical storm I ever see'd. Sky full of lightning bolts. Clouds a banging. Then, pow! And in a flash, young Jesse wuz gone !"

Time hadn't changed Corky Tabor much. His tasseled hair was now gray, his whiskered face wrinkled. But, he still spoke with animated hand movements, and could yet make a bottle of wine disappear in a flash.

"What happened to the body?" asked Jeremy Wade.

"T'wern't no body," replied Corky.

"No body?"

"We never found a body," verified Adam Quayle who was a rookie officer in 1959, and the third member of a three officer police staff headed by William Bo Brennan. Jeeter Potts doubled as file clerk and dispatcher with a police rank of sergeant.

"Isn't that a bit strange?" asked Jeremy, referring to the lack of a body.

Pykes Pit was a strange place. Over the years, the worked out, gravel hole played host to many bizarre events that smacked of Twi-Light Zone influence. The Jersey Devil once visited the pit to save a fair maiden from a train robber named Leroy Pykes, for whom the pit was named. Legend has it that Pykes brought a chest of gold coins here one summer night, when the pit area was yet woodland. Pykes and a cohort, Billy Rice stumbled onto the coins while robbing a sleepy train en route from Atlantic City to points north.

They lifted wallets and watches. They took a young virgin hostage, and tossed a rebel conductor to the wind. They then invaded the baggage car to find the metal-lined box stowed beneath a pile of canvas mail sacks. The chest had been loaded aboard by a beachcomber who dug up the booty along the Brigantine coastline - buried there by the infamous Black Beard back in the Seventeen Hundreds.

"Dad, the agent here might have another appointment waiting," said Charlton Tabor II.

Stopping the train, Pykes stood guard while Rice went for a cart to transport the treasure back to their lair. Each rail car teemed with bobbing faces. Thus, Pykes did not notice a fleet-footed brakeman slip away to flag down a county sheriff already in the saddle. The horse and the cart arrived together - from opposite directions.

A gunfight broke out.

Pykes killed the lawman, and hitched the cart to his horse. Rice took a shoulder bullet from an on board detective waiting for an open shot. Pykes returned the volley, and the railroad guard fled to get reinforce ments. Before a posse could form, the bandits vanished into the pine lands where Pykes finished off Rice for his share of the gold, and raped the girl, whose name was not made public record. Pykes then setup camp and began to count coins.

"Dad please," whispered Tabor Jr trying to curtail Tabor Sr's colorful tale.

Blue mist filled the air the story goes, when a terrified boy puffed into town and told of un- earthly sounds coming from the campsite. The young hobo said the screams were human, but the growls sounded animal. Authorities returned to find nothing but a bloody finger, pulsating amid some eerie hoof prints, etched in trampled soil. Natives believe the Jersey Devil made the prints. Natives say the devil slew Pykes, rescued the distraught maiden, and buried the gold.

Jeremy Wade hid a slight smile as he listened to Corky Tabor's hand-animated yarn.

Adam Quayle stared blankly at Corky's son, Charlton, who coughed slightly and looked away.

Somebody bought the story.

Shortly thereafter a hole appeared at the campsite. Then a second hole appeared, and a third. At the onset of the post-war building boom, a contractor named Lucas O'Leary brought in a front-end loader and finished the job up brown. Endless loads of foundation dirt rolled out to the meadow lands for a housing development called Bayside Glen. The digging left a cavity big enough to bury the national debt.

The gold never turned up.

Nor did the rest of Pykes.

"Eerie things can happen in that Pit,"   said Corky.

"Yes, I can see that,"   said Jeremy Wade.

The infamous Elmer Kane killing took place in the pit. The 1958 murder case centered around a bow that law enforcement failed to find.

A year later, Jesse Joe Jacks disappeared.

County Sheriff, Eugene Baker Sr had deputized Jacks to spearhead a renewed search for Helena Ann Hollister. The unsolved case was then a year old. Mrs Rodney Hollister, along with the murder weapon were still missing at that time.

Lieutenant, Emmet Walker Thomas called for action. The Lower Elk county detective maintained that Rodney Hollister was innocent, and the key to the killing lie with his wife.

Jacks started the search in the pine lands where local authorities found Hollister's Venetian Red Corvette. The trail of course was cold. Jacks then went on a bow search around Pykes Pit, where Jacks vanished without a trace.

QUANTUM ROOTS

"Maybe someone should check the basin floor for quick sand," suggested Jeremy Wade.

"We did that while investigating the Helena Hollister case," said Adam Quayle, "We even checked a good bit of the topside area."

Pykes Pit lies roughly two miles northeast of Lake Powhatan, and some fifty yards inside a weaving Lower Elk Township border. To the south west run the Atlantic City power lines that feed civilization to the desolate pine lands. To the northwest stretches the Elk County Game Forest. The forty square-mile tract provides free camping, fishing and hunting. Rabbit and deer are abundant. Random rifle shots can be heard year 'round, despite a New Jersey State gaming timetable. Often, a folded doe gets quickly crammed into a ready car trunk. Occasionally, a poacher gets collared by the county game warden.

"Seems like just yesterday when Jesse Joe was that warden," reminisced Corky Tabor as the black hearse left the graveyard, "And God help those poachers. Jesse was as mean to people as he was soft with animals. Came back from Korea that way. Don't exactly know what happened over there. Something about shooting live bodies that wuz frozen. Didn't talk about it much."

"I understand you were as close to Jessie Joe Jacks as anyone," said Jeremy.

"We shared a beer pitcher now and then at Grogans," replied Hobbs Creek's first hobo, "Went to grammar school together. I dropped out after the eighth grade while Jesse went on to Mt Loyal High."

"Anything else you can tell me about Jacks?" asked Jeremy Wade.

"He played the piano."

"He played the piano?"

"Yessir and he always wore cleats on his boot heels," said Corky, "I always suspected he wanted to sound bigger than what he was."

"He was small in stature?" asked Jeremy.

"No sir," said Corky, "He just wasn't tall."

"The vigilante in this film clip appears tall," said the special agent.

"Jesse also wore risers," said Corky.

"Risers?"

"Boots with elevator lifts," explained Corky, "Makes a man look two or three inches taller than what he really is."

Get back to the pit, Jeremy, texted Alexis.

"What else can you tell me about Pykes Pit," asked the special agent.

QUANTUM ROOTS

Today, the rusty slopes are impregnated with tire tracks from trail bikes. Smelly trash and want-me-nots litter the sticky basin floor. No Dumping signs are everywhere. Trespassers are stiffly fined if caught. In the late fifties, mutilated targets plastered the pit walls. Targets that were fired on by tournament sportsmen and local police officers seeking gun qualification. Jesse Joe Jacks used those targets to tweak his gun shooting skills.

"Best damn shot that ever lived," wheezed the elder Tabor through chattering teeth, "I watched him one time put a bullet through a bullet hole. A'int too many people who can do that."

Well, that explains the marksmanship, texted Alexis, *Move on to the data.*

"My data bank says you were born in 1926," said Jeremy Wade, "Since you and Jesse Joe Jacks schooled together, that would put Jacks somewhere in his late eighties."

"Yes, Sir," replied Corky, "Jesse Joe would be pushing ninety. He wuz one grade ahead of me, even though we had the same teacher."

"So here's the problem," said Jeremy Wade tapping his video screen, "This film clip shows the vigilante to be in his early thirties."

"Yes, Sir."

"Yet, you positively identified this man to be Jesse Joe Jacks."

"Yes, Sir."

"Based on what?"   asked Jeremy Wade.

"Based on that facial mole," replied Corky Tabor pointing at the leather face on Jeremy's smart phone, "Soon as I see'd that lip mole, I knew that wuz Jesse Joe."

"There are other men with a lip mole,"   said the junior agent.

"How many of them men shoot left handed and can pick a flea off your nose without drawing blood," said Corky Tabor,   "How many of them men can cut the bulls-eye out of a range target."

"You eye witnessed this man shoot in a range tournament?"   asked Jeremy Wade eager to hear more about Jacks' gun shooting ability.

"No sir, when Jesse Joe showed up for a shoot out,"   cackled Corky ,   "Everybody else went home."

"That good, huh,"   said Jeremy.

"Jacks was barred from local competition,"   said Adam Quayle,   "Jesse was somewhat demoralizing to the other contestants.   For what it's worth, I once watched Jacks give a fast draw demonstration right there in Pykes Pit. He flipped a dime skyward, drew and hit the coin in mid-air. An onlooker picked up the dime and there was a hole, dead center."

"That's good," said Jeremy.

"That's good," echoed Adam Quayle.

"Thank you for your help, Mr Tabor," said Jeremy who then offered condolences over Corky III. As Adam Quayle pulled from curbside, Jeremy looked back to see Charlton Jr steer his father into a warm sedan. Jeremy then looked down as a text message returned from Alexis Grumman.

We need another opinion, Jeremy.

CHAPTER 6

Darkness fell as the two lawmen exited Chief Adam Quayle's black and white squad car, and climbed into Jeremy Wade's unmarked government issue. The special agent used emergency flashers and mucho patience to exit the police lot and break through the crowded sidewalk.

"Where's your bubblegum light?" asked Adam Quayle.

"Somebody copped it," replied Jeremy.

"Along with your foot cast?"

The junior agent smiled, "It was due to come off two days ago."

"I could have driven," said Quayle, "I still have some night vision left."

"I've got department equipment in the trunk," replied Jeremy Wade, referring to media convertors they would need for the job ahead, "Unfortunately, I'm not a geek."

Keep your two-way on and I'll help.

Roger that, Alexis.

You don't address me as Alexis, soldier.

Roger that, General.

QUANTUM ROOTS

The two lawmen drove southeast out of Hobbs Creek until swamp smell gave way to salt air. They sped past some new high rises and parked under an awning that read: Shady Rest Nursing Home.

A white clad attendant answered the buzzer.

The multi-level care center served the able bodied, the disabled and the senile. Thus, doors were locked to prevent certain patients from wandering into the street. A solemn desk clerk looked up saying, "He's waiting for you in the video room."

"This is Jeremy Wade," said Quayle motioning toward the special agent.

"Adam, do something with Bo Brennan," said the female desk clerk.

"Like what, Gladys?"

"Adam, the man doesn't belong here," said the bitter desk clerk, "He's disruptive. Nobody likes him. He growls at Maggie."

"Maggie the matron?" inquired Adam Quayle, feinting surprise.

"And sometimes he barks at her."

"He barks at her?"

"Like a dog."

"I'll talk to him," promised Quayle, "We need the key to the sound closet."

Reluctantly, the desk clerk pulled a key ring off a peg board. She explained that the gold key unlocked the sliding door, the silver key opened the video cabinet. She handed over the keys saying, "If anything happens to the wireless mikes, it's my hide in the sling. We have patients who love to relive radio days, like Old Man Porter who wheezes through here making sounds like Inner Sanctum."

"Henry Porter?" said Quayle, "The Henry Porter from Grogans Bar & Grille? The Henry Porter who nips at fire trucks and tried to commit suicide by jumping off a stepladder? The one with the wart on his nose?"

"The same," replied the desk clerk, "We hide him when new applicants show up. He's bad for business. Also, we find playgirl magazines under his mattress."

"You mean playboy."

"No, playgirl."

"You do have your hands full," said a smiling Adam Quayle as he headed off with Jeremy Wade in tow. Quayle carried a laptop. Wade held a bag of connection cables. The cafeteria, kitchen and sitting lounge were grouped together just off the Shady Rest main lobby. There was a library, workout room and hair salon scattered throughout the four wings. The two lawmen found former Police Chief, William Bo Brennan strapped to a wheelchair in the video room. A white cast wrapped his right foot. Maggie The Matron stood by.

Said Adam Quayle, "We need to modify your sound closet to show this video. We must make the RCA jacks compatible with a USB port."

Jeremy, is there a sale on foot casts somewhere? asked Alexis Grumman over the FIC video network.

So you do have a sense of humor, replied Jeremy to multiple screens back in the operations room. Wade's special issue transmitter could capture multi-directional footage which kept real time video between Alexis Grumman and the junior agent.

Is this the right William Brennan? asked Alexis.

Ten Four, replied Jeremy.

He appears to be asleep, said Alexis

"He tried to kick out the back door," said Maggie The Matron explaining the cast on Bo Brennan's foot, "Then he blew cigar smoke in my face so I could not sound an alert."

"Why doesn't that surprise me," said Adam Quayle as Jeremy Wade entered the sound closet.

Continued Quayle talking to Maggie The Matron, "Rest assured we will leave everything the way we found it.. .and Bo. ..I think you'll find this film clip interesting, if not a bit unbelievable."

"I'd like to shove that yellow whistle up her ass," muttered the ex police chief.

I don't think he's asleep, whispered Jeremy into the two-way.

"Did I ever tell you about that bear I bagged," asked Bo Brennan addressing Jeremy Wade.

"Not now, Bo," said Adam Quayle.

"It was me and Bucky Harris that caught up to him," said Brennan, "Ole Bucky was president of the Belly Snakes Hunting Lodge back in those years, He had his trusty Winchester. I had my double ought six."

"Not now, Bo," said Adam Quayle.

There was a day when William Brennan ran the show in and around Hobbs Creek. The good folks addressed Bo as Sir. The bad guys trembled. Brennan took the Top Cop position on December 4, 1949. He was given one part-timer to man the radio during rush hours, and allotted some black and white paint for his private car. The pay was meager, but benefits good. And, it was a short drive to work because Brennan's living quarters doubled as the Hobbs Creek police station. Over time, Brennan became the focal point of Corky Tabor's fore mentioned bar room tales, and somewhat fishy smelling stories.

"I find it unbelievable that a law officer would smoke a cigar in a nursing home," said Maggie The Matron.

"Law officer retired," corrected Adam Quayle who signed on as a Brennan prodigy in 1958. A local building boom turned farmland into housing, and city fathers voted to beef up the two man police force. Quayle and two other hopefuls took a civil service exam in Mayor Willard Green's basement office. Quayle won the job with high score of 92. His GI Joe haircut helped. Afterward, Adam Quayle went through two more interviews and eight weeks of academy training.

It was a time before home computers, micro chips and social media. TV shows were black and white, cars sported tail fins and the hottest technology on the planet was the integrated circuit. Adam Quayle now studied a remote control device loaded with tiny buttons that performed a variety of mysterious functions. He turned to yell toward the sound closet, "I can't get this screen to come down, Jeremy!"

"Push the *watch* button," called back Jeremy, "The screen should come down."

Take your two-way out of your pocket, and I might be able to help, said Alexis texting the junior agent.

I like having you in my pocket, replied Jeremy texting back.

Jeremy, that's uncalled for, and we're on duty
Yes Ma'am."

"We weren't really after bear," continued Bo Brennan watching a blank wall, "We were tracking deer. Bucky took an early shot and winged this eight-pointer. Course, once you wound them, you gotta find 'em. You know that."

The movie screen housing hovered over a empty wall just opposite the video beam that projected from the sound closet. The white canvass was programed to lower when the operator pressed the selected mode button on the remote controller.

"Anyway," said Brennan waiting for the screen to come down, "We gave the thing a little run-out time, then we started to track. And what a chase. Two or three hours. Zigging, zagging. All the time headed for the river. Then as the prints got real fresh we came around this bluff, and here's a bear. Bigger than life. He stood on the cliff just at the waters' edge. You had to be there, Jeremy. He weren't no farther away than that spare wheel chair. And he wasn't black. He was brown. And it's the brown ones that test your gravel. They will chew up a man and never stop to spit out his ammo belt."

"Push menu," called out Jeremy getting info from Alexis, "Then select the *screen down* option."

"Stare him down was my first idea and that's what I did," continued Brennan watching the screen come down, "Froze him with a look while I got my rifle in position. Then I aimed for right here. This is where you gotta hit 'em. Right here in the rib cage. This is the kill zone. And wham! Got him with one shot. And when you gun for brown bear, that first shot better count. You go wounding a brown bear and you are in some deep shit"

"Bo, there's a lady present," reminded Adam Quayle referring to Maggie The Matron.

Is the screen down? texted Alexis.

Screen's down, replied Jeremy, *What's our status off duty?*

Zero, texted Alexis,

"I think Bucky took a shot too," concluded Brennan, "But Bucky's shot missed."

Brennan's shot missed, high to the right. And Harris only nicked the bear in the leg. The startled animal toppled off the cliff, free fell some 'hundred feet and crashed into a floating timber log.

What's the holdup? texted Alexis.

No picture, texted Jeremy, *I think the USB port is faulty.*

Jeremy, listen to me close. Put the flash drive in the USB port. You should have a printer cord with an audio cable attached. Use this cable to connect the laptop to the wall jack marked projector and no we are not having dinner, tonight.

I didn't ask, replied Jeremy.

You were going to. texted Alexis.

The projector was programmed for DVD and VCR. Jeremy's movie clip formatted to computer video. Jeremy needed to transfer the film content onto the big screen to accommodate Bo Brennan's failing eyesight. This made it necessary to use the outdated movie equipment. Alexis solved that problem by interfacing a laptop with the air cooled projector.

Texted Alexis Grumman to Jeremy Wade, *You should be up and running.*

"We've got lights," called out Jeremy, "You're up Adam."

Said Quayle addressing the screen, "The two gunmen boarded the bus right at rush hour. One bandit pointed a gun at the driver's head, while his accomplice robbed the passengers. They didn't know the bus was armed with a security camera. . .Jeremy, the screen just went back up!"

Alexis, the screen just went back up, whispered the junior agent.

Reboot again and you don't address me as Alexis.

Dinner tomorrow night? asked Jeremy.

No ! replied Alexis.

Minutes later, the screen lowered. Continued Adam Quayle, "The two gunmen appear to be teens trying to cultivate a beard, Not only did they overlook the camera, they also failed to see the vigilante seated nearby. . .Jeremy, the screen just went up again. .no. .wait .it just came down again. . .no, wait. .it's up again."

"I think Mister Brennan nodded off," said a second nurse joining Maggie The Matron.

"Jeremy, this screen is out of control!" yelled out Adam Quayle

"I think he's done more than nod off," said Maggie holding her nose while checking Bo Brennan's plastic diapers.

"I think you're right," agreed the second nurse now holding her nose.

Jeremy? texted Alexis Grumman.

Yes, boss?
Find another witness.

CHAPTER 7

Two days went by. The vigilante struck three more times, grabbing headlines away from high food prices and world wide, market crashes. One shooting incident involved a local councilman's son caught robbing a filling station. The vigilante peppered the get-away car, which crashed into a gas pump and the whole station burst into flames.

Under renewed department pressure, Jeremy Wade found Winfred "Woody" Herman inside a Carson City shooting gallery named Targets. The indoor pistol range catered to hunters, gun enthusiasts and local police officers seeking re qualification. Herman was a hunter.

"I'm going to show you a short video clip," explained Jeremy Wade, "You might find it a bit graphic."

"I'll try and handle it," replied Herman stuffing a Remington 223 back inside a rifle case.

Targets Shooting Gallery spanned the width of ten lanes. Each alley ran seventy-five foot deep and included an automated target return. Six lanes were designated for handguns, and four for rifles. Pistols could be no larger than 44 caliber, rifles no bigger than a twenty two. Growled Herman, "I'd like to use my 30-30 in here, but rules are rules and at least I'm out of the snow."

"I need you to ID a face," said Jeremy Wade bringing up an image on the two-way.

Woody Herman pointed to the wide shot group on his paper target and mumbled that the weapon was too light. He exited the stall and led the special agent onto the tiled show room floor. Said Herman, "The lighting's better out here, and it's a bit more quiet."

Rifles lined the inside wall of Targets' display room. Handguns and head wear filled a row of smudgy glass cases.

Targets opened in 1927 as a wholesale outlet for hunters. The adult westerns of the fifties sparked a renewed interests in handguns. Targets began stocking small arms. Then, the peace beads of the late Sixties weighed down revolver sales, and Targets moved the hunting rifles into the handgun cases. The peachy lovey thing wore thin by 1980, and cowboy guns returned, including the remodeled Colt 45.

"And that's what this appears to be," said current owner, Benjamin Wheeler as he studied the cell phone video that Jeremy showed Woody Herman. Continued Wheeler, "I didn't catch your name, agent."

"I'm special agent Wade," said Jeremy.

"This is special agent Wade," said Woody Herman taking a look at Jeremy's credentials.

"I'm Benjamin Wheeler," said Benjamin Wheeler, "I bought this store right after 911. America was ready to re arm, and I wanted in on the ground floor. So let's see what you got from the beginning."

Jeremy ran the short video clip from the point where the two armed youths boarded the bus. As the film ran, Wheeler turned his ball cap around backwards, and let out a low whistle. The vigilante appeared from the rear of the bus. He blew up the one boy's gun, then disarmed the second boy with a wrist shot that dumped the unfired weapon onto the bus driver's lap.

"Holy shit," gasped Wheeler with burly arms folded, "That sonofabitch just put a bullet into the barrel of that kid's gun. It's a miracle it didn't blowup in the kid's face. Who the hell can shoot like that?"

"That's what we need to find out," replied Jeremy, "I was hoping you could identify the shooter."

"None of my members shoot like that," said the gun shop owner, "Don't allow that kind of gun play in here, anyway.."

Targets Shooting Gallery posted a full bulletin board of firearm rules. Quick draw and hip shots were prohibited, along with circus tricks such as shooting between the legs, while facing away from the target. Failure to comply with Wheeler's rules led to a one year loss of club privileges. A second offense meant dismissal. Concluded Wheeler, "I take firearms serious as you can see, agent. A weapon better be unloaded when it comes through that door, and it better be empty when it leaves the firing line."

"Very commendable," said Jeremy Wade.

"Maybe it's bogus," said Woody Herman tapping the screen on Jeremy;s two-way.

"Bogus?" queried Jeremy Wade.

"Tricked out film," replied the Belly Snake president, "Maybe somebody's seeking attention on TV or You Tube."

"Maybe," said Agent Jeremy Wade staring at a dusty ceiling fan running in slow motion, "However, our technicians took this footage right from the bus security camera."

"With due respect, agent," said Woody Herman, "We have all had weapon training. This film reeks of Hollywood. Nobody can fan a single action 45 off the hip with any kind of accuracy. This is a put up job."

"I have to agree," said Benjamin Wheeler, "Put this film in real time and the vigilante shoots himself in the foot."

Later, back in DPA Headquarters:

"First off, the vigilante's firearm is not a single action Colt 45," said Bernie Miliquist pointing to a spot on the giant video screen, "This weapon is a double action, Smith & Wesson ACP 45. It holds six shots and the trigger both cocks the hammer and releases the hammer."

Bernie Miliquist was a *special projects* instructor for the Federal Intelligence Center, located just off the Virginia, Eastern By Pass. Occasionally, the F.I.C. would employ a civilian with expertise in firearms, karate, explosives and various forms of self defense. Miliquist specialized in light weapons and air rifles. He stood now in the main projection room, and critiqued this latest vigilante sighting, while sipping coffee and toying with the screen pointer. General Alexis Grumman sat cross-legged on a folding chair. Jeremy Wade stood nearby with cell phone open, and eyes on Alexis.

Jeremy, you're peeking up my panties.

I've never seen you in a skirt before.

Stop texting and look at the big screen, Jeremy.

Yes, Ma'am.

'Let's examine the holster next. . .if I can have your attention," said the special projects instructor, "The holster is not some sort of break-away movie prop. This holster is a modified Jordan used for fast draw, cowboy shooting. Notice how the gun handle tilts away from the hip. This allows the shooter to lift the weapon away cleanly without jamming the barrel,

"Also notice, there's no real change of speed throughout the vigilante's draw. Just one smooth motion from start to finish. And, our vigilante does not hip shoot, nor does he fan the gun. Instead, he braces his firing elbow against his solar plexis. This is his horizontal sight. Simultaneously, he brings the other hand over to the weapon, and uses an eyeball and the free index finger as a vertical sight. This latest video reveals a lot because the vigilante stands directly beneath the camera while being filmed."

Dinner two nights from now? texted Jeremy.

No, and stop peeking up my panties!

I'm not peeking up your panties, texted back Jeremy who had already seen the clip a half dozen times.

Earlier, this candid camera film came to federal attention via a civil liberties union, who claimed local authorities were standing aside due to public support for this new folk hero. The FIC reviewed the case and ruled against deploying a federal swat team. Thus, the vigilante sightings would stay with the department of paranormal activities, under director, Alexis Grumman.

My pants suits are in the cleaners, Jeremy.

Can I check your closet ? texted Jeremy.

No !, texted back Alexis.

"If we can play the film one more time," said Bernie Miliquist facing a screen that went blank, "I'd like to point out something else that often gets missed by the untrained eye."

"Doug !" called out Alexis, "From the top !"

This latest vigilante film documented the demise of the Purple Dragons, a Mt Loyal street gang that terrorized waterfront residents from Bridge Street to Harbor Yacht Landing. The incident played out on a Saturday evening. Busy boaters tied cabin cruisers to galvanized deck clasps. Their female counterparts dressed for a dinner date at the nearby Water Front Inn.

Suddenly, seven armed youths burst into the basin with guns aflame. Those in the open, dove for water. Those below deck, crouched to cabin floors.

Screams filled the brackish air.

Cell phones frantically called 911.

Enter, Jesse Joe Jacks.

"Stop the film here," requested Bernie Miliquist as the vigilante stepped from the shadows and nailed six of the seven youths in rapid succession, "Note the distance between targets. Now, notice the vigilante's horizonal movement is executed by twisting on the balls of his feet, while his neck, waist and hips are kept locked in position, Again, vertical alignment is done with eye and a pointed index finger. This is known as Point Shooting."

Alexis, what's Point Shooting? texted Jeremy.

Doug, what's Point Shooting? texted Alexis.

I'll check our data banks, texted back Doug.

Bernie Miliquist learned Point Shooting from a hand book written by Bobby "Lucky" McDaniel, a 1950's icon who taught fast draw and hip shooting with an air rifle. McDaniel found that slow moving BB's were visible to the naked eye, which made it possible for the student to track *hit* and *misses.* Such an aid enabled the armed novice to quickly move from the conventional sight picture, to the mind's eye.

Added Bernie Miliquist, "Many of Lucky McDaniel's students were bird hunters, target shooters and police officers of that era. Choice of gun made little difference. McDaniel could teach anyone to shoot anything. He even worked with the military. And, he always began with a short demonstration to establish he was the real deal."

"Could we get that short demonstration?" asked Lieutenant General, Alexis Grumman.

"I thought you would never ask," said Miliquist freezing a small smile.

The Federal Intelligence Center maintained an *on-grounds* pistol and rifle range, where agents re-qualified with their issued weapons, annually. The six lane gallery lay behind the motor pool, just east of the main building. Alexis led the way wearing the uniform skirt that failed to cover her long legs. Now and then, she would pause to yank the hem downward.

Bernie Miliquist followed, walking briskly for a senior citizen out on social security, but still working the odd job here and there.

Jeremy brought up the rear, dragging a new foot cast that covered a fractured ankle, re-injured when he stepped in the same pot hole. Jeremy blamed a missing rabbits foot for the mishap. Alexis Grumman merely sighed and bit her tongue.

"Some say I'm double dipping," said Miliquist talking to Alexis, "I call it getting what I'm due."

"And wise you are," replied Alexis.

"Sprained ankle?"   noted Miliquist looking at Jeremy's foot cast.

"I missed the bad guys with a Judo kick and damaged a steel pole,"   explained Jeremy.

"I fractured my ankle once,"   said the special projects instructor,   "Stepped into a pot hole. Why aren't you out on workman's comp?"

"Jeremy used up comp time when he fractured his wrist,"   said Alexis, dryly.

"And that was another adventure,"   bubbled Jeremy,   "I missed my target with a Karate chop and put my hand right through a wall !"

"You lead an exciting life," said Bernie Miliquist.

Once past the motor pool, a sandy trail forks off the bumpy service road and heads due east. Down range angles away from the Interstate, putting the shooter's back to traffic noise. The trio stopped in front of six paper-covered targets backed up by a gravel slope.

"This will be a two part demonstration," explained Miliquist strapping an open top holster onto his right leg. He loaded six bullets into a 22 caliber revolver, and slipped the double action handgun into the low riding holster. The sun would be no problem thanks to some hazy cloud cover and good range planning. Continued the firearms tutor, "We will start off with some known distance shooting, briefly called K.D, "

Last chance for dinner, Alexis,

Jeremy, I don't date younger men with foot casts and you don't address me as Alexis.

Ten four, General and for what's it worth, your ass is showing.

Jeremy !

Bernie Miliquist squared off with the first target, He stood with feet spread 18 inches apart, knees flexed. He drew without warning. Six shots rang out in three seconds. He hit all six bulls-eyes.

Jeremy and Alexis fell suddenly silent.

"It's nice to have your attention,"   said Bernie, "Now we move on to objects in flight. The key here is to practice with colored BB's so the shooter can observe flight patterns. First, shoot ahead of the target, then purposely shoot behind the target. Eventually, the subconscious mind will find the center."

The small arms instructor put away the air gun and reloaded the twenty-two. He pulled a yellow tennis ball from his tote bag. He lobbed the ball skyward with his left hand. He shot the ball out of the air with his right hand. Next, he ran the demonstration with a golf ball, then asked for a dime.

"You are kidding," exclaimed Jeremy Wade.

"You toss it and I'll hit it."

Bernie Miliquist was good to his boast. Seconds later he blew the floating coin out of the air.

"Holy cow!" exclaimed Jeremy.

"How many people can shoot like this?" asked Alexis upon finding her voice.

Bernie Miliquist unloaded the weapon and packed all props back into his tote bag. He fingered the gray mustache beneath his tiny nose and went on to explain that gun clubs like CAS and SASS have bred some top notch marksmen.

"CAS stands for Cowboy Action Shooting," said Bernie, "SASS is the Single Action Shooting Society. Both clubs require contestants to shoot against the clock, and fire weapons reminiscent of early America."

"I had no idea this movement existed," said the DPA director, "Briefings must have took place before I came state side."

The renewed interest in hand guns began on the west coast in the 1980's, then gradually spread across the nation. Hollywood type stages were built for these would-be cowboys. Back drops depict scenes from

86

yesteryear. Props require the marksman to stop a bank robbery, draw against a cardboard silhouette, save a fair maiden, etc. Cash prizes are rare, ribbons plentiful. But, contestants do have the chance to become crack shots.

"And crack shots can become expert in *point and shoot* methods," said Bernie Miliquist.

"How many of these crack shots would use a large frame weapon like a forty-five?" inquired Alexis noting that Miliquist's arsenal consisted of BB's and lightweight Twenty Two's.

"Anybody who grips the gun with both hands can use a large frame gun," replied Bernie, "I use light weapons because I shoot with one hand. My index finger points at the target, my middle finger pulls the trigger. The vigilante holds the gun with two hands. One index finger sights the target, The other index finger pulls the trigger."

"So, he's not really fanning the weapon," said agent Jeremy Wade.

"He's not," said Bernie Miliquist.

"So, we're not necessarily looking for someone with giant hands and burly forearms?" asked Alexis.

"I'm afraid your vigilante could be just about any body," replied the special arms instructor.

Twenty four hours later, Deputy Director, James Iron Horse Taylor pulled the plug on the vigilante investigation. Taylor swamped the case for lack of evidence pertaining to paranormal activity.

Lt General Alexis Grumman moved on to a UFO sighting over the Grand Canyon.

Jeremy Wade was temporarily assigned to a desk job, counting paper clips and sorting rubber bands.

Part Two

CHAPTER 8

Ten days remained before Christmas. Snow continued to fall. Shopping lines grew longer, tempers shorter. The six-o-clock news highlighted road rage incidents, and warned of sub-zero temperatures by morning. A cheerful weather girl was advising motorists to stay home *if at all possible,* when Olan Chapman burst through the front door of Cabin Eighteen.

"Olan ?" said Ivy Chapman looking up from a noisy vacuum cleaner..

"My rabbits," cried the slender computer geek who went missing a week back.

"Olan !" gasped Ivy, suddenly realizing her husband was home.

"My rabbits need to be brought inside !"

"Screw your rabbits !" screamed Ivy Chapman,

"Where the hell have you been !"

Olan Chapman strode through the four room dwelling and swung open the kitchen door that led to the frozen back yard. He stood legs apart in dirty jeans, and opened the top button on a tattered flannel shirt. He stared out over Lake Powhatan as his troubled eyes scanned the immediate area,

"Your rabbits are in the spare bedroom," said wife Ivy as relief melted anger, and questions replaced profanity. After a few fuzzy answers, Ivy said, "A phone call would have been nice when you came out of that coma."

"Where's the Timothy Hay?" asked Olan Chapman, inspecting the cabinet that stored the rabbit food.

"On order," replied Ivy, "And why are you wearing a mustache, you hate mustaches."

"On order?" muttered Olan Chapman, "I don't understand *on order.*"

"Maryann Grundy has been taking me shopping. Where she goes doesn't carry rabbit food, so I ordered it online."

"Duffy opens early," said Olan, "I'll get a bale in the morning."

"Who's Duffy," asked Ivy.

"Duffys Meal & Grain," said Olan.

Mostly, cabins at Lake Powhatan use compact appliances. Washer and dryer units are stacked. Refrigerators run campground size, as do hot water heaters. Cabin Eightteen was no different. There was enough hot water for one bath, and Ivy gave that tub-full to Olan Chapman, who refused to walk naked through the cabin. Ivy shrugged off her husband's odd behavior, and called the Hobbs Creek Police Station.

"I didn't know he was missing," said Isabel Jackson referring to Olan Chapman.

"Isabel," asked Ivy Chapman, "Is Adam there?"

"No Ma'am."

"Is Jeeter Potts there?"

"No Ma'am." said the Hobbs Creek dispatcher as she hit the speaker phone button, and resumed filing long purple nails, "I think Jeeter's down at Fishers Pond. Word has it he either teaches the grand kids to ice skate, or he sleeps on the sofa."

"Isabel?"

"Course, I don't know why he cares at his age."

"Isabel."

"Yes, Ma'am?"

"Are you chewing gum?"

"Yes, Ma'am."

"Well, take the gum out of your mouth so I can talk to you," said Ivy Chapman,, "I promised Adam a call when my husband showed up. I don't know where the bastard's been, but he's back."

"Yes, Ma'am."

"And Isabel?

"Yes, Ma'am?"

"You can erase my profanity off the tape."

"Yes, Ma'am."

"And Isabel," said Ivy Chapman, "Where's Duffys Meal and Grain Store."

"Ma'am, we have no listing on any Duffys Meal and Grain store."

"Are you sure?"

"Not in this county," said the Hobbs Creek dispatcher.

Duffys Meal & Grain supplied oats, mash, hay and assorted items for farm animals throughout Hobbs Creek Township and Lower Elk County.

The onetime supply center for livestock closed in November of 1960.

CHAPTER 9

County Sheriff, Eugene Baker Jr showed up at Cabin 18 the next morning. The puny son of former sheriff, Eugene Baker Sr, stepped from the unmarked car and cursed as roof top snow dropped into the open collar of his brown uniform. Shuddering, he helped a weak defroster clear the rear window, and then keyed off the engine.

The house number to Cabin 18 was nailed to the top step of an open porch. He kicked the snow clear to make sure the number read 18 and not 16, before knocking.

The solid front door opened a crack.

"I'm looking for an Olan Chapman," he said

"Aren't we all," said Ivy Chapman.

"Ma'am?"

"He's not here."

Baker took folded stationary from an inside pocket and waved it at the narrow slot, saying, "This is a summons for Olan Chapman to appear before Judge Anthony Pelligreni on charges of reckless driving, demolition of county property, etc etc etc."

"He's not here."

"There was a message on my machine this morning from Police Chief, Adam Quayle, to the effect that Chapman was here,"   said Eugene Baker Jr.

"He was here,"   replied a half dressed, Ivy Chapman swinging the door wide open for Baker to peer inside,   "The bastard left sometime in the night. Don't know when. I got up and he was gone."

Sheriff Eugene Baker stood on tippy toes to peer over Ivy Chapman. The front room was clear, as was the kitchen. He had no way to check out the bedrooms. Said Baker,   "Do I have to go back for another court order?"

Ivy Chapman pulled her robe closed tight. She scrutinized the Lower Elk County lawman and glanced over the summons. She strode to the kitchen saying, "Want some hot chocolate?"

"Never touch the stuff,"   said Baker looking around,   "Makes my gut curdle."

"Coffee then,"   said Ivy,   "This is one of those one cup wizards that spits out a variety of flavors including just plain coffee."

" What's with the rabbits?"   asked Baker

"Olan has some strange ways,"   said the sleepy-eyed woman,   "Some times I think he prefers pets over people. Especially tall people. Olan is very jealous over tall people."

"So, that explains the elevator shoes," said the county sheriff poking through the bedroom closet, "He didn't say when he would be back?"

"He didn't say he was leaving," said Ivy, "And I don't think he would be hiding under the sink."

"I have to be thorough," explained Baker, "A small man could hide in a cabinet."

"Sheriff!" cried Ivy Chapman, "Olan's not a midget for chris'sake!"

Truth be, size was also an issue with County Sheriff Eugene Baker Jr who taped in at 5'-8" and weighed a mere 160 lbs. Baker's father, Sheriff Eugene Sr stood 6'3" and tipped the scales at 235 lbs. His stature alone commanded respect with jail birds and county work gangs. Eugene Jr's authority came from a gun and a badge. The tell-tale signs showed up in his swagger, and a voice too deep for his shallow chest cavity.

"We have an animal ordinance in this county," said Baker, "We also have a livestock ordinance."

"Meaning what?" asked Ivy.

"Those rabbits have to go," said Baker.

"You do realize they will freeze to death out-side," said Ivy.

"I'll send animal control out to get them," said Baker.

Ivy Chapman made her coffee and put the second cup away. She stared coldly at the county sheriff and flatly said, "Next time, bring the proper papers,"

Eugene Jr. finished his search by checking under the front porch. He found nothing but a burlap sack and a rubber doggie bone. Satisfied the mister had flown the coop, he grunted a thank you to Ivy for her patience and climbed into the unmarked squad car.

"And thank you for tracking snow through my house," said Ivy bringing in a frozen news paper, "Come back when you have time for a doughnut."

CHAPTER 10

The white delivery truck backed to the rear door of Club Cinema Cinder. The truck merely read Delivery because additional writing faded to oblivion. A blue clad driver jumped out. Bridge noise sounded overhead. The Manhattan skyline loomed in the distance. The driver pushed a bell button marked for deliveries.

No answer.

He pounded on the steel roll-up door.

No answer.

Frustrated, the driver loaded four boxes onto a hand truck and legged it around the block. He ducked under the droopy awning of this Big Apple night spot and backed through the double front doors. Strobe lights and flashing bodies filled the dance floor. Here and there moved a person who looked almost human.

The delivery man stopped at stage front and glared at the band. The bass drum read Fatina And The Clowns. They were five in number including the drummer who appeared to be in another dimension.

The driver motioned to the lead singer for whom the band was named.   She was an Egyptian with jet black hair and dead white skin. She wore a purple slit dress that hid a rubber penis strapped to her mid drift. Periodically, she would flash the penis and scream *UP YOURS*, which always brought hysteria from this homo sexual crowd.

The driver held his ears and pointed to the boxes. The singer pointed to a side door that led to the back. Seconds later, the singer and the drummer joined the driver in a dimly lit room, loaded with costumes and sound equipment.

"Where's Shack?"   asked the driver.

"Shaykh is dead,"   replied Fatina.

"Who's this?"   demanded the driver nodding toward the drummer.

"This is my cousin Caliph,"   said Fatina as the drummer removed a rubber mask and a red wig,   " He can be trusted."

"Me and Fatina used to sleep together,"   said the drummer giving the singer a steamy look,   "Then one night mother caught us naked under the high bed. Mother got very angry and sent Fatina to live with cousin Jamal."

"Quiet Cal,"   ordered the girl.

QUANTUM ROOTS

Caliph Farouki's parents took in Fatina Farouki after the 1992 earth quake that fiercely shook Cairo, and left cousin Fatina an orphan. It was one of those *right theater, wrong highway* moments. Fatina's parents were en route to Opera Square when a giant tree toppled onto their cab, killing them and the cabbie. After which, Caliph's parents gave Fatina food, shelter and some classical sheet music.

The teenage Fatina did own great voice range. Fatina's parents once hoped their daughter would be another Umm Kulthum, known in Arabic circles as The Star Of The East. Sadly enough for the Farouki family, Fatina swapped Raq el habib for songs such as Walk Like An Egyptian, a Yankee pop tune. That, coupled with the bed incident was the straw that broke the camel's back.

"I don't like this," said the driver.

"Neither did the camel," said Fatina.

"Who the hell's talking about a camel," said the driver edging closer to the exit door.

Fatina opened the cargo. Two tassels hung down her back, split by a woven hair braid. Her high heels looked like cock roach killers. A dozen neck laces glittered as she pulled a drum from each of the three boxes. The cocaine hid in some chrome frame work.

She tasted the white powder and tossed a wad of bills to the driver as she said, "Maybe you will like this better."

"I would like to do my business with Shack," insisted the driver.

"I don't like drugs," said cousin Cal, "Drugs are bad for me. I always just say no to drugs."

"Hush Caliph," demanded Fatina who then spun on a heel and said to the driver, "Shaykh died on a staircase back in Virginia, I'm taking the messages now."

Fatina And The Clowns originally came under the direction of Shaykh al Azmad from Islamabad, Pakistan. Azmad and Fatina met while attending Quaid -i-Azam University which is located in Islamabad. They both spoke perfect English - partially because the college blossomed on the Yankee dollar, and partially because English is Pakistan's official language. Fatina attended the public university to find a wealthy man, while Azmad pursued a career in computer science, which required a four year degree.

Those were the Good Times for Azmad and Fatina. Each semester ended with a vacation break, and each vacation led to a new playground - on the ole man's money. Azmad liked Monte Carlo and the lure of

Baccarat, among other casino games. Fatina chose Cancun beaches and Caribbean cruises. Laughter came easy. Sex bubbled like champagne at the captain's table.

The hayride ended October 7, 2001. Nine-One-One now over, retaliation against al-Qaeda began. The United States forces coupled with British military launched *Operation Enduring Freedom*, a mission to remove Afghan territory as a safe haven for terrorists. Caught unaware, Azmad's parents visited relatives in Kabul when the bombs fell. Kabul is the capital of Afghanistan, another land of kings and vagabonds. No one in the wealthy al Azmad family survived. This left Shaykh with a heavy bankroll, and a revengeful thirst against the United States - and all other coalition forces that worked with the Northern Alliance.

T'was the beginning of America's war on terror, and the end of a fun seeking college student.

The twenty four year old, Shaykh al Azmad soon met an insurgent named Dim Lyt al Qassum who wished to restructure an earlier version of the Black Hand. However, Al Qassum lacked the finances to fund the five member, terror teams. Thus, he viewed Azmad as a gift from Allah. Not only could Azmad finance deserted training camps from Pakistan to Turkmenistan, but the former college student spoke with the charisma needed to convince Afghans that religion justifies murder.

Eventually, Azmad formed the colorful band to promote his terrorist activities against America. He devised the *paper message system* to avoid satellite detention by the F.I.C. The system was elementary. A courier would carry the message from Shaykh to various computers with remote ISP addresses. Messages returned the same way. Thus, Shaykh's realtime location never showed up on a GPS.

Ultimately, the band served a two-fold purpose. The innocent clown image also reduced scrutiny while crossing International borders. However, fate can be strange. Custom officials were not al Azmad's waterloo. Fatina became his undoing. The icy lead singer shot Shaykh al Azmad in retaliation for a lost brother, who died at the hands of Martin Swan and the Invisible Six.

"They are bad men," explained Caliph to the courier, "They drowned cousin Kary."

"They didn't drown Kary," said Fatina giving Caliph a black look, "They fed Kary to an alligator and I'm holding Martin Swan responsible for my brother's death."

"I don't know of Martin Swan," said the courier.

"You will," said Fatina, "Martin Swan is why you are here."

"I want to deal with Shack," said the courier.

Fatina pulled a 32 from her handbag. She pointed the cold barrel at the courier's head and said, "Maybe you would like to join Shaykh."

A knock came on the dressing room door. A voice demanded that Fatina and Caliph return to the stage. Fatina grabbed a folded note from the courier. The message read: *Martin Swan. Jodie Swan. Tonight. 5pm. Carson City/Hobbs Creek landing strip. Black SUV. Tenn license plate. Partial No. 246.*

Fatina put a lit cigarette butt to the wrinkled note. She dropped the flaming paper into a metal trash can, and unlocked the top drawer of a filing cabinet. Shaykh al Azmad worked in units of five. Each member of the cell commanded another five member unit. Shaykh al Azmad had kept personal stationary that identified him to his next in command. Fatina adopted the same format. She tore a sheet off the purple pad and hastily scribbled: *Bring this Martin Swan to me. Kill everyone else.*

"*Everyone else* could include the messenger," she said staring coldly ahead.

The driver looked from Fatina to Caliph to a fresh money roll coming his way. He said, "No body shoots the messenger."

"I do," said Fatina. "In or out?"

The driver grabbed the money. His was halfway out the door when Fatina waved her message like a paper flag in a wind storm. The driver returned for the purple paper note and disappeared.

Fatina smiled. She returned the unloaded thirty-two to her handbag. She grabbed Caliph by a chunky arm and headed for the restless audience.

CHAPTER 11

"Quad City pilot, this is tower."

"This is Quad City Challenger II."

"This is tower. You are leaving Atlantic City air space. We are turning you over to Mt Loyal.. . . Happy landing."

"Roger that,"   replied Eddie Thompson flying blind through a snow cloud. Poor visibility had almost scrapped his 4pm, scheduled take-off. Now, conditions grew worse as he flew over Lower Elk County.

"Crazy Eddie,"   whistled the traffic controller at Mt Loyal Municipal Airport. He looked up as the tan dem, two-seater flew overhead. Continued tower,   "I'm glad you are not bringing that bucket of bolts down here."

"Don't be a wise ass, Jay,"   said the 41 year old pilot for hire,   "What am I looking at?"

"Another six inches,"   said tower,   "Winds up to thirty-eight miles an hour. Coming out of the northeast. Temperatures predicted to hit zero by midnight."

"Roger that."

"How's the new baby?"

"Looks like his mother," replied Eddie.

"So the kid gets a break," said tower, "One more thing."

"Yeah?"

"The power might be out ahead."

"Roger that," replied Eddie.

Edward Gerald Thompson was on a mission. His job was to transport Melvin Swan back to Atlantic City, where the Democratic congressman could be flown to Washington DC for a senate investigation inquiry. Thompson was picked for the transport job because the one-time dare devil owned the only available ski plane within a tri-county area.

Thompson built the ultra light glider to replace his Challenger One, which he lost to a rather tall tree top while on a transport job. Miraculously, Crazy Eddie walked away with little more than a black eye. His fare died.

Undaunted, Thompson borrowed thirty-three thousand dollars and built Challenger II to keep his *taxi by air* business going. The plane was a top wing, with the engine behind the cockpit and some tripod landing gear beneath the aluminum framework. Top speed clocked in just under 100 mph, and range petered out somewhere around 250 miles.

He pushed a communication button three times and welcome lights lit up the lone Hobbs Creek run way. When the lights appeared as white and red, Eddie brought the plane in. A pre fab hangar sat at the end of the snowy lane. A black SUV waited in the parking area. Two unmarked cars hid in nearby wooded areas.

Eddie knew the SUV carried his fare, Melvin Swan. What Eddie didn't know was that each olive drab car held a dead government agent. One man slumped over the steering wheel. The second man lay back against a blood-stained seat. Both men were here to guard Congressman Melvin Swan from a possible mob hit. Both agents had been killed with a 9mm handgun, execution style.

"What's wrong?"   asked Patricia Thompson from the far end of Eddie's cell phone.

"The office door's open."

"And?"

"Pete never leaves the office door open,"   said Crazy Eddie plowing toward the ominous hanger,   "And there's no lights on. Even the bathroom. The light's always on in the bathroom. That's one of Pete's biggest gripes. Nobody ever turns out the bathroom light."

Peter Townsend owned Kirbys Air Service which sat east of Hobbs Creek proper and straddled the Hobbs Creek /Carson City boundary line. The rural air strip was founded in the roaring twenties by a George Kirby, who catered to crop dusting planes - and a few wealthy hobbyists with an eye to the sky, and a head in the clouds.

As farmland turned to housing developments, demand for agriculture spraying fell off. Kirby sold out to Townsend, who realized change was in the air. The pocky faced entrepreneur ditched the local farmers, and picked up some mosquito spraying jobs from Lower Elk County. He coupled the local contracts with some gypsy moth treatments required by the state – and presto – Kirby air traffic was back in business.

Crazy Eddie climbed out of the cockpit and headed toward the hanger.

All was dark.

All was still.

Snowy footprints led to each of the government cars, and back to the hanger door. Eddie knelt down and traced a forefinger around an indentation. The print was made by a leather shoe, not a rubber boot. Muttered Eddie into the cell phone, "There's supposed to be some federal guys around here somewhere."

"Federal guys?" queried Patty Thompson trying to stir soup, hold a baby, talk on the phone and collar a fleet-footed Eddie Jr, simultaneously.

"And I don't see any sign of the congress man," said Eddie Sr.

"What congressman?"

"The congressman who's a mob hit target ."

"Eddie!" cried Patty Thompson, "What the hell are you into now?"

Earlier, a federal contact promised Pete Town-send a hefty bonus to air lift Melvin Swan out of Lower Elk County, which was the congressman's home district. Townsend struck a bargain with Crazy Eddie who was scheduled to return from Atlantic City before dark. Now, the fare was here, the hangar doors were wide open, but the money was nowhere in sight.

Shivering, Eddie stepped into the blackness.

His eyes adjusted to the shadows.

"Oh shit," he said.

"What is it?" asked Patty over the cell phone.

Pete Townsend lay draped over the wing of a single engine, Cherokee. His pocky face tilted upward. His open eyes stared without seeing. Blood soaked his work uniform and trickled onto the dirt floor.

"Eddie, get out of there!" screamed Patty.

A muffled shot sounded.

Eddie saw the flash. He felt the bullet. He clutched his chest and fell forward onto a drop cloth.

A gunman walked from the shadows and stood over Eddie. The gunman was Mid-Eastern descent. His dark eyes flashed triumphantly. His stubby face twisted into a grin that looked like a rumpled bed. He paused with the 9mm pointed downward as though waiting for his victim to move.

The cell phone now screamed from the dirt floor.

Eddie raised his head. He clutched the soiled drop cloth and reached for the phone.

The gunman shot Eddie again.

Eddie continued to squirm.

The shooter placed the gun barrel to Eddie's neck and fired.

The body died.

"Allah has struck!" cried the gunman into the cell phone, "Praise be to Allah !"

"Who is this !" screamed Patty from the far end of the line, "Where's Eddie ! I heard gun fire! Put Eddie on the phone1'

Outside the hangar, the runway lights had turned off. The gunman fumbled through a giant fuse box on a back wall of the cinder block building. He finally found the right breaker and the whole area lit up. Melvin Swan waited in the black SUV. The gunman pulled the congressman from the car and pushed him spread eagle over the snowy hood.

"Suh, I take it you're not one of the good guys," said Swan.

"Quiet !" ordered the gunman speaking Arabic. He handcuffed Melvin Swan and shoved the befuddled congressman into the rear seat of the tandem designed, snow plane.

"And somehow I sense you're not a hit man for the mob," said Melvin Swan, "And I sense this has nothing to do with my congressional hearing in Washington."

"Quiet !"

"Well, does it Suh?"

The gunman swung the plane around to face the runway. He shut down the radios and turned on a private two-way. He continued to praise Allah as he cried, "I have Martin Swan !"

Terror sometimes brings on giggles. This be one of those moments. Melvin Swan's grayish eyebrows raised. His dark eyes twinkled. His red bow tie began to bobble. Soon, the black man broke into laughter.

"You find this amusing?" asked the Arab.

"I'm not Martin Swan," said Melvin Swan, "You have bagged the wrong bird."

"You lie !" cried the Arab, "All westerners lie !"

"Martin Swan is a white man," tooted the congressman from Lower Elk County, finding strength in the sound of his own voice, "I'm a black man. I'm sure even you camel jockeys can tell the difference."

The gunman looked confused. Gradually, confusion turned to worry. His bushy eyebrows furrowed. His black eyes darted about as though seeking an answer. He opted to chance a message. He snapped a picture of Melvin Swan and attached it to a text. He hit the *send* button.

The two men waited

The message would have to go through a runner to reach Fatina, then return the same way. A long hour later, the answer came back.

Fool ! You have the wrong man.

"And now for the real bad news," snickered Melvin Swan, "You need to do an about-face and look out the wind shield."

Some 100 yards down the runway, stood the vigilante. Feet spread. Left hand hanging loose below his gun holster. White snow speckled his black hat brim, as swirling wind beat against his weathered ammo vest.

QUANTUM ROOTS

He looked like a page from yesterday.

The terrorist cursed and swung the yellow, ski plane on a collision course with the vigilante. Howling wind grew louder as taxi speed picked up. The wing struts shook. The tail rudder shuddered. As the two adversaries drew close enough to lock eyes, the vigilante drew his side arm.

Six shots rang out.

The first five shells took out the plane's front landing ski. The nose section dipped. The middle east pilot now became a sitting duck behind the panorama windshield.

The sixth shot hit a patch of black hair between the Arab's eyes.

"You give all them virgins a big ole howdy for me," said Congressman Melvin Swan as the pilot fell forward into the elevator stick. Blood squirted onto the odometer. The tee tail lifted and sent the plane into a barrel roll. The nose cone hit the runway, which put the plane in a three point stand.

And that left Melvin Swan hanging over the dead terrorist.

CHAPTER 12

"Well, he's suing us, Frank."

"Ed, he can't be suing us," said Mount Loyal Police Chief, Frank Cantene.

"Frank, the congressman was handcuffed in the rear seat," replied City Mayor, Ed Morrison, "When the plane went nose down, he spent three hours suspended over a bloody corpse. Eventually, the EMS boys got there and cut him down."

"But the vigilante saved his black bacon."

"Frank, this is today's world," reminded the Mount Loyal City mayor, "Everybody sues everybody. People would even sue The Pope."

"But the gunman was a terrorist !"

"Frank, terrorists are politically correct," said Mayor Morrison, "Vigilantes are not. So far, I've had calls from Swan's lawyer, the NAACP, the civil liberties union, an ambassador from Pakistan, and some spanish speaking person from HUD."

"Hud !" screamed Frank Cantene out the open window, "What the hell does urban housing have to do with this?"

QUANTUM ROOTS

"Your Honor," interrupted Agnes Blackwell who was the mayor's secretary, "Pedestrians are listening."

The Mount Loyal City Police Station sat next door to city hall. The mayor's office window faced the police chief's office window. When the two civil servants boiled over, they would lean over the weathered sills, and yell at each other across the alleyway.

The girl friday lowered the window and set up a phone connection between the mayor and the police chief. Simultaneously, the two men plopped into their respective phone chairs and lit a calming cigar.

"I'm sorry now I closed the window," muttered Agnes Blackwell

"So Frank," drawled the Mount Loyal mayor staring at a busy ceiling fan, "What are we doing other than eating donuts and checking seat belts?"

"Ed, we have a name," replied Frank Cantene.

"I'm listening," said the mayor.

"Jesse Joe Jacks."

"I don't know any Jesse Joe Jacks."

"Jacks was our county game warden back in the Fifties," explained Cantene, "He was struck by lightning in the summer of fifty-nine."

"And?"

"He died," said Cantene.

"He died?"

"According to Corky Tabor," replied Chief Frank Cantene, "Tabor claims Jacks disappeared in a sudden flash while standing in a gravel hole named Pykes Pit. Tabor claims there was quite a bit of water covering the basin floor at the time."

"Who's Corky Tabor?" asked the mayor.

"Our records show Charlton Tabor to be a connoisseur of wines, whiskey and cough syrup," mumbled Frank Cantene.

"Frank."

"Yeah, Ed?"

"You got anything else?"

Mount Loyal City had a roll call of 550 homeless living inside city limits. Carson City coupled with Hobbs Creek counted a few less than that number. All three police departments were leg weary from checking dumpsters, park benches and back street missions. Concluded Chief Frank Cantene, "We believe these street people are harboring this Jesse Joe Jacks."

"The dead guy?"

"The dead guy."

"Frank, I know the media is fascinated with this one man cowboy show. Your department is fascinated with this self appointed judge and jury. You're taken with this vigilante. I'm not, and I mean to take action."

"But Ed," replied Chief Frank Cantene, "This guy saved Otto's life."

"Who the hell is Otto?" demanded the mayor.

Lower Elk County was currently midway through a four month sting, code named *Operation Meal Deal.* The multi agency investigation encompassed, Mount Loyal City, Carson City, Hobbs Creek, unincorporated farmland and portions of the Pine Barrens. Participating law enforcement agencies included city, county, state, Homeland Security and the United States Dairy Association.

Police Lieutenant, Joseph Ottoman went under cover for Frank Cantene and the Mount Loyal Police Department. Otto was the officer of choice due to drug bust experiment, plus an unkempt appearance that resembled a hobo.

The purpose of *Operation Meal Deal* was to crack down on fraudulent food stamp use, by small grocery stores, back street gangs, drug dealers and any John Q Public person willing to commit Social Welfare Fraud. Current estimates place annual food stamp expenditure at $72 billion, with a 1% fraud percentage.

In this case, the stamps took the form of a $300 debit card issued by The Office Of Inspector General, along with correct pin numbers. Joseph Ottoman's job was to entice an unsuspecting shop keeper to purchase a card for $150, thus doubling the store's investment at cash-in-time.

Eventually, Ottoman's disguise wore thin. He had just delivered a mini-market's second refill card, when three gunman waited for him in the back alley.

One man hollered *Hey Copper.*

All three men drew weapons.

Ottoman was unarmed, his car and gun waited a block away. His choices were few. Talk his way out of this death trap, or run. Neither option held much hope.

Then came help.

"Three shots rang out in less than a second," said Chief Frank Cantene, "All three gunmen fell to the snow, instantly. Otto turned. The vigilante was gone."

"This dead guy," said the mayor.

"Yes, the dead guy," said Frank Cantene,"

"Frank, you got 48 hours,"

"Ed, I can't promise you apprehension within that time frame," pleaded the police chief, "This vigilante flies under the radar."

"You got 48 hours," repeated the mayor.

Over the next four days, the vigilante struck three more times. Two convenience store robbers fell victim to *the fastest draw in the east.* A car thief had the wheels shot from beneath the stolen vehicle.

Then came the icing topper.

A hooded intruder held up City Bank which sat directly across from city hall. The hold-up man had a helicopter stashed on the roof of a nearby high rise. As the daring, daylight crook attempted a get-a-way, the vigilante showed up. Shots rang out. The copter flew into a dizzy spin, and dropped on top of the mayor's red roadster – which was illegally parked on Main Street.

The mayor and the police chief now waged another face-off across the alley way.

"You won't be laughing when I pull your freaking badge," cried Edward Morrison out the open window.

"Sir, please return to the desk phone before the sash falls on your stomach," said Agnes Blackwell with a coaxing arm grab, "We don't want another meat wagon ride do we."

"Ed, I spoke with Adam Quayle," said Frank Cantene after Morrison picked up his desk phone, "You remember Quayle, he's the police chief in Hobbs Creek. He took over for Bo Brennan some years back. We now have some new evidence."

"I'm listening," muttered Morrison.

"This vigilante doesn't think he's a outlaw," said Frank Cantene.

"The dead guy?"

"Yes sir the dead guy," said Frank Cantene, "This vigilante thinks he's a lawman. He might even envision himself as a Wyatt Earp."

"Wyatt Earp?"

"Kinda like a Wyatt Earp."

"Frank."

"Yeah, Ed ?"

"Is this freaking Dodge City !"

"No, Sir."

"I'm calling the Feds," threatened the mayor.

"Just bear me out Your Honor," said Police Chief Frank Cantene, "Quayle claims that Jacks was deputized just prior to being killed by the lightning bolt that Corky Tabor witnessed. Records do show that Jacks was deputized to track down suspected killer, Helena Hollister."

"Who's Helena Hollister?" asked the mayor.

"Rodney Hollister's wife."

"I remember that case," said Agnes Blackwell, "The Hollisters vs the Kanes. Money against money. Put Hobbs Creek on the map. And that poor Elmer

Kane. Choked to death on his own blood."

"Could we cut to the chase here," said Mayor Edward Morrison.

"Archives show that Mrs Hollister was a New York City gold digger who vanished somewhere in the South Jersey Pine Barrens," said Frank Cantene.

"Kinda like your second wife," said Agnes Blackwell talking to the mayor.

"Hush Aggie," said Morrison, "Go on Frank."

"Anyway," continued Cantene,, "Jacks failed to find Helena Hollister. However, Quayle can't remember Jacks ever turning in his badge. Consequently, Quayle feels that Jacks just might believe he's still a bonofide lawman."

"The dead guy."

"Yes, the dead guy."

"Frank?"

"Yeah, Ed?"

"I'm calling in the feds."

CHAPTER 13

Special agent Jeremy Wade hobbled up the entrance steps to FIC headquarters.. He paused at the top plateau to catch a quick breath and rest his injured foot, weary from dragging an ankle cast up the concrete risers. Heavy highway fumes drifted over from the Eastern By Pass. Diesel horns and sirens cut through the early morning air.

"I see your cast has switched feet,"   said the icy door guard as he checked Jeremy's ID chip with a body scanner,   "Same pothole, Sir?"

"Stanley, you're not funny," said Jeremy,   "You can remember busted bone locations, but can't recall that I belong here."

"Just doing my job, agent."

Jeremy pointed toward the sirens and flashing lights and asked,   "What happened ?"

"Another pile-up in that low area,"   said the security guard,   "We have summer fog and winter flurries. It all rings up money for ambulance chasers and you need to hurry along, the lieutenant general is waiting."

"Thank you for the head's up,"   said the special agent,   "And that brings us to more irony. This building operates with a Top Secret scenario. We have body scanners, hand print screens, security cameras, encrypted passwords. The Director's policy states that everything said in a briefing, stays in a briefing. Yet, you seem to know everything that's going on."

"Easily explained,"   said the bony MP with the giant ears and protruding Adam's Apple,   "I'm the seventh son of the seventh son."

"Of course,"   said Jeremy Wade,   "Why didn't I think of that."

"Now, I'll give you something else to think about,"   said Stanley while adjusting an itchy arm band.

"Please do,"   said Jeremy.

"This vigilante you're chasing might not be a man,"   said Stanley.

Jeremy paused by the revolving door that led to the second check point that led to the third check point. He turned and stared at Stanley who continued saying,,   "The vigilante just might be a woman."

"Female?"   asked Jeremy.

"Most women are female, agent."

"Our vigilante seems male,"   said Jeremy,   "It's nice you think outside the container, though."

"I think *box* is the word, agent."

"Whatever," said Jeremy Wade disappearing into the building.

"You're late, agent," said Lt General Alexis Grumman as Jeremy eased the ankle cast through the security door that opened into the inner DPA office.

"I got caught in that traffic jam," said Jeremy.

"That's bullshit," snapped Alexis, "You come in from the other direction.

"Would you believe I got into a kick boxing bout with a bearded man on a camel," said the junior agent pointing toward the new foot cast.

"I would believe you stepped into another pot hole," said Alexis Grumman.

"Roger," replied Jeremy Wade taking note that the deputy director's lips were again colorless, "I guess that lip stick thing didn't work out ? "

"Jeremy, we shared dinner last night because we were temporarily off the case," said Alexis, "Also, snow warnings were on.. .and... I happen to like that little waterfront restaurant. It reminds me of back home. Especially that homemade spaghetti sauce."

Back home for Alexis Grumman was almost any spot on the globe. Her service oriented father went periodically from army base to army base. Often, the move would be overseas. Thus, Alexis grew up with no real roots, just spotted memories here and there. The Casa de Mia reminded her of a small eatery outside of Rome, where the teenage Alexis went agog over a dark haired waiter with long eye lashes, and a dimpled grin. Jeremy reminded Alexis of that waiter.

"Understood," said Jeremy, "You started to tell me about a son?"

"I had a boy out of wedlock," said Alexis, "I named him Skip in memory of his father who vanished before I left the maternity ward. That was a long time ago."

Alexis Grumman's father was stationed at Ft Benning Ga. when the teenage Alexis became pregnant by a corporal platooned on Sand Hill. Desert Storm was just heating up. By the time Alexis left Martin Army Hospital, the baby's father was AWOL somewhere in Canada. Grabbing boot straps and sucking it up, Alexis began her own officer training right there on Main Post. Over the next two decades, she toted Skip Jr on a military career that would encompass the globe.

"He's almost your age," said Alexis.

"Understood," replied Jeremy, "So why are we back on this case?"

"Doug, bring up those two screen images." said the deputy director, using the pause to swallow an aspirin with water from a small paper cup. She gagged, complained the water was warm and said to Jeremy, "The vigilante finally screwed up. He reloaded after killing the terrorist back at the Hobbs Creek/Carson City airstrip. Then, for whatever reason, he left the empty shell casings on the runway."

"The blue light is out," said Jeremy Wade,

"What blue light?' asked Alexis.

"Your water's warm because the cooler's un-plugged," explained the junior agent, "The cord's laying loose behind the unit. Just plug it in and hit the reset button."

"Thank you, agent," said Alexis Grumman.

"You must have been running late, yourself," noted Jeremy, "It would appear you left your bra home."

The deputy director buttoned her open blouse and snatched the pointer from an oblong conference table. She directed the fiberglass rod toward the wall screen and said, "Can I have your attention up here, Agent,"

"Yes, Ma'am."

"We dug these casings out of the runway snow," said Alexis Grumman pointing at a split screen image, "We didn't get much, but we did get this one partial thumb print. And this print matches the print we have on file for a Korean War veteran,"

"Jesse Joe Jacks?" asked Jeremy Wade.

"Jesse Joe Jacks," confirmed Alexis..

"Stanley has a thought," said the junior agent.

"Stanley our door guard?"

"The same," said Jeremy Wade, "Stanley thinks the vigilante could be a woman. . .or maybe a transvestite who dons heels and a dress after each shootout, and then melts into the female population."

"Jeremy."

"Yes, Ma'am?"

"Stanley plays pocket ball."

"Yes Ma'am," said the junior agent who conceded they were back looking for a guy who died fifty years ago. Then studying a vigilante image on the giant screen, Jeremy asked, "What's with the star pinned to his vest?"

"That badge ties to the Elmer Kane murder case," explained Alexis.

"And that links to Helena Hollister," said Jeremy following the director's thought trail.

"According to Sergeant Jeeter Potts," said Alexis Grumman, "Jacks was deputized to find Ms Hollister. When the case went to the back burner, the badge was never turned in. . .at least that's the way Potts remembers it. And that coincides with testimony from Hobbs Creek Police Chief, Adam Quayle. We just got that information from Mt Loyal Police Chief, Frank Cantene."

"So, we're looking for an outlaw who thinks he's a lawman," mused Jeremy Wade.

A room buzzer went off. Alexis walked to the outer office and returned with a fax folder. She opened the manila cover and said to Jeremy Ward, "You're on a first name basis with Adam Quayle. Is he solid or soupy?"

"Solid," replied Jeremy.

"And Jeeter Potts ?"

"Don't know," said Jeremy.

"But they both believe that Jesse Joe Jacks is the vigilante," said Alexis looking for confirmation.

"Adam told me that the vigilante is a carbon copy of Jesse Joe Jacks," said Jeremy, "Adam calls it spooky. . . . real spooky."

Alexis Grumman tapped the picture of the star pinned to the cowboy vest on the big screen. She said,

"Both men are sure that Jacks was deputized. However, neither man remembers the badge being returned. I faxed this recent vigilante picture to the Hobbs Creek Police Station. Both men identify this star as the badge that never came back."

"That's creepy," said Jeremy.

"Needless to say," said Alexis, "Our lab men would love to get their hands on this star, as much as we'd like to question this vigilante."

"I have a question," said Jeremy, "Since the vigilante believes he's a lawman, why doesn't he just come forward?"

"Kutzman has some thoughts on that," said Alexis.

"Our resident head shrink?" asked Jeremy.

Alexis nodded saying, "Dr Kutzman thinks this guy is a fish out of water. Maybe spooked. A man from yesteryear, thrown into today's cyber space world."

"But you don't think so," said Jeremy Wade..

"I don't believe in quantum leaps or magic carpet rides," said the Lieutenant General, "There's another answer here somewhere. . a logical answer. . .we need to find it."

The junior agent paused by the door and watched his female boss bend over to fill a paper water cup. He gave a playful whistle and asked, "Dinner tonight?"

"No," firmly replied Alexis Grumman, "Put your dreams in your pocket, Jeremy."

CHAPTER 14

A rusty oil drum and a broken down bulldozer have welcomed visitors to Pykes Pit for the past fifty years. Often, fallen tree limbs or a nosy pine snake will block the winding entrance road. Heavy foliage delays the dawn. Dense fog lingers in low areas. On this particular wintry day, snow was the problem.

"Jeremy, I hope your seat belt's fastened," said Alexis Grumman over the car's speaker phone.

"So you do care," said the junior agent as he clutched a clammy steering wheel, while sliding wildly through snow drifts.

"Jeremy, the car is signed out to me."

"I love you, too," said the junior agent.

"Jeremy, we are not an item."

"Stanley the doorman thinks we are."

"Stanley the doorman belongs on daytime television," said the Lt General as she watched a small dot move across the GPS screen back at FIC head--quarters, "And I hope you're obeying all traffic laws. We incur enough trouble with local government."

Jeremy Wade didn't own a private car. His transport choice was a motorbike. His mishap list was an arm long, including an international incident when he collapsed a sidewalk cafe outside a Madrid, bull fighting ring. Jeremy never nabbed the bad guy, but headquarters caught the bill. Currently, Alexis pushed the right insurance buttons and got Jeremy - and his foot cast – into a department car.

"I see the parking lot !" cried Jeremy clearing the woods and squinting at the sun kissed snow.

"Jeremy, that's not a parking lot !"

"Looks like I have the place to myself," said the junior agent barreling toward an opening on the horizon.

"Jeremy !" screamed Alexis, "Brake now ! I say again, soldier. Brake now ! "

Suddenly, the obvious became the obvious. Jeremy shoved the rubber pedal to the floor board. The olive drab car slid to a stop seconds before going over the cliff. The rear wheels stayed on the ground. The hood section extended outward like a small bridge that led nowhere. Jeremy Wade gasped relief. Then, came the jitters like rolling waves of tide water. The basin floor appeared to be a mile down. The driver's door post creaked. The chassis began to slide forward.

"Jeremy, tell me that image I see is not the car hanging over the cliff," muttered Alexis over the car speaker.

Silence.

"Oh shit," said Alexis, "That image is the car hanging over the edge of the cliff."

"I think I need a cigarette," said Jeremy.

"Jeremy, you don't smoke."

"But if I did, I would need a cigarette."

The passenger door creaked. The chassis slid forward another foot.

"Jeremy, listen up," said Alexis, "Roll over the seat. Exit by a back door. We can replace the car."

The chassis slid forward another foot.

"I hope we have a backup plan," cried Jeremy releasing the seat belt. He grabbed a head rest and hoisted his foot cast over the top. He hit the back seat as the car rolled off the cliff.

"Jeremy !" screamed Alexis.

"Oh shit," cried Jeremy.

"Oh shit," murmured Alexis.

The olive drab car with the solid black tires raced down the fluffy slope like a missile on a mission. Wind whistled, snow flew. The vehicle hit the basin floor, bounced into a wild spin, and slid across the ice into a snowbank.

All fell silent.

"Jeremy?"   whispered Alexis.

No answer.

"Jeremy !"   cried Alexis.

Still no answer.

Suddenly, the junior agent let out a scream.

"Jeremy, what is it?"

"There's a face at the window."

"What!"   exclaimed Alexis.

"I think it's Big Foot."

"Jeremy, keep the window up."

"He wants to talk,"   said Jeremy checking himself for cuts and bruises. Satisfied he had no broken bones, he cracked open a back window. Icy eyebrows appeared, followed by a ruddy nose, red from too much booze, and a mouth with too few teeth. It wasn't Big Foot. Nor was it the Abdominal Snowman or the Jersey Devil. Jeremy lowered the window. He flashed his ID badge and said, "We've had reports of gunfire coming from this basin."

"Weren't me,"   replied the hobo looking about the empty canyon, "That was a real nice piece of driving. How did you do that from the rear seat?"

"That's classified,"   said the junior agent.

"Of course," said the hobo, "I really thought you were going to flip the car over. Guess that's all part of your G-man training."

"I'm not on a training mission," said Jeremy.

"Then you must be looking for moonshine."

"What's your name?" asked Jeremy.

"Timothy J. Harper," said the hobo, "The jay stands for Junior and I'll give you a tip. We don't make moonshine in gravel pits."

"What are you doing here, Mr. Harper?"

"Mostly, staying out of the open air," said the hobo, "That northeast wind can freeze a man on the spot, and no one will find you 'til the spring thaw."

Smiling, Jeremy slid behind the steering wheel. The smile turned to a frown when the sluggish engine failed to start. A few attempts later, Timothy Harper took the driver's seat. The hobo held the gas pedal to the floor, turned the key and the engine roared into life.

"We have heat," cried Jeremy Wade, "How did you do that?"

"Back in my healthier days," explained the hobo, "I owned and operated Junior Harpers Garage & Towing. Had some pretty big jobs, too. Fetching flipped over tractor trailers and such. And I can tell this, son. You're probably looking at five grand to get this crate out of this basin."

"Jeremy, is that Timothy J. Harper?" asked Alexis Grumman over the speaker phone.

"This is Timothy J. Harper," replied Jeremy.

"That's Timothy J Harper?" asked Alexis.

"Sir," said Jeremy turning from the phone to the hobo, "Are you Timothy J Harper?"

"I'm Timothy J Harper," said the hobo.

"Alexis," said Jeremy, "We're all in agreement, this is Timothy J Harper."

"Who's that talking?" asked the hobo.

"That's my boss," said Jeremy.

"You work for a woman?"

"I work for a woman."

"Do you ever poke her?"

"No, but I'd like to."

"Jeremy !" screamed Alexis over the car phone, "We can hear you two back here at headquarters . . . and you don't call me Alexis !"

"Yes Ma'am."

"Jeremy?"

"Yes Ma'am?

"Go to text."

"Ten four."

QUANTUM ROOTS

We have a file on a Timothy J. Harper, texted Alexis, *He might be a link to Jesse Joe Jacks. Try not to spook him. Harper, I mean.*

I think we're safe on that one, texted Jeremy.

Timothy Harper was eight years old when he watched Abel Johnson set up the infamous murder scene at Pykes Pit. Harper's schoolyard chum, Jodie Herman failed to witness anything because he left his glasses home. Harper's story fell on deaf ears because the boy was under age. Neither boy ever witnessed Abel Johnson or Helena Hollister with the murder weapon. Neither boy saw the kill shot that dropped Elmer Kane. However, Timothy Harper was now among the few alive who remembered a Lower Elk County game warden, named Jesse Joe Jacks..

Jeremy, show him the picture, texted Alexis over the two-way.

"Is that some kind of secret code?" asked the hobo sneaking a peek at Jeremy's two way.

"I'm going to show you a photograph," said Jeremy Wade to Timothy J. Harper, "It might be a bit unsettling. Just take your time. You don't have to make an identification if you are not sure."

"Boy, the way you revenuers work," said the hobo, "It's almost eerie. I'm not in the moonshine business, myself. Never touch the stuff. I did have an uncle though, who ran a still not far from here. Uncle Jeb. On my daddy's side. Died young from his own whiskey."

"Bad batch?" asked Jeremy.

"No, the storage tank fell on him."

"Mr Harper, we are not from the federal division of firearms and alcohol," said Jeremy, "We are from the department of paranormal events."

Show him the picture, Jeremy.

"Yeah, that's him," verified the hobo looking at the face on Jeremy's communicator, "That's Mr Jacks."

"You mean that looks like him," suggested Alexis switching to speaker phone.

"No Ma'am," said Timothy Harper, "I mean that's Mr Jacks."

"How can you be so sure?" asked Alexis.

The hobo traced a forefinger over the face on the communicator and said, "This lip mole is why I'm so sure. Only Mr Jacks had a lip mole right there."

"Timothy, do you know a Charlton Tabor?" asked Alexis Grumman.

"I know a Corky Tabor," said the hobo laughing, "Can't remember ever calling him Charlton."

"The vigilante sightings have dominated the news media," said Alexis, "Have you and Corky discussed this vigilante?"

"Not hardly," said Timothy Harper, "I haven't seen hide nor hair of Corky since we wuz in the tank, together,"

"And when was that?" asked Alexis.

"Don't rightly know," said the hobo, "About a year ago I reckon. Chief Quayle can tell you. He's the one fished us out of the drainage ditch. Drunker than a skunk. Corky hit the numbers and we wuz really tying one on."

"Timothy, this is Alexis Grumman," said Alexis, "I'm the DPA director for the Federal Intelligence Center. I would like to ask you a few questions that go back to 1958."

"Yes, Ma'am."

Pykes Pit was shaped like a gigantic peanut in 1958. Thus, shooting distances varied from 75 to 250 feet. Harper remembered that Jesse Joe Jacks would move from lane to lane, shooting the bulls eye out of each target. Harper also reinforced previous testimony that Jacks was so superior to other marksmen, that the Elk County game warden was prohibited from local gun tournaments. Harper recalled one incident where Jacks shot the word *beer* out of a beer can.

"Well, that coincides with our other accounts," said Alexis Grumman, "This Jesse Joe Jacks must have spent a lot of time at Pykes Pit."

"He did," said Timothy Harper, "His cabin's not that far from here."

At the word *cabin,* Alexis Grumman and Jeremy Wade went suddenly quiet, together.

"Cabin," exclaimed Alexis breaking the silence, "Of course Jacks would live in a cabin. He would live in a cabin in the woods."

CHAPTER 15

The Jersey Pine Barrens skirt Pykes Pit to the north. This infamous wasteland is rich in folkways and folklore. City dwellers who leave the main road for a shortcut to the ocean, often vanish in these gloomy woods. Much of the 1.3 million acres is uninhibited, and if you stay lost long enough, the countless sandy trails that lead nowhere, begin to dig tiny graves in the mind.

Alexis, my phone battery shows red, texted Jeremy Wade hobbling up Lost Trail.

You need to power up, Jeremy. Look around for a convenience store.

I don't think you are getting the picture, Alexis.

Natives say the mafia bury victims here. Whiskey stills, outnumber houses. Buckshot often echoes through trees, and Jersey Devil stories are numerous. Also, there's this place called Quicksand Pond that takes the rap for missing runaways, and AWOL husbands. But, the most colorful yarns tell of a 40 foot pine snake, owned by a horseshoe player named Ian Dixon, who lived in a camper and survived on fish and deer meat. Fellow campers swear the reptile stretched the entire length of the horseshoe court. Witnesses claim the snake was also part rattler and part Boa Constrictor, with the ability to match color to surroundings.

The story goes that when Dixon was in a tight game, he would let loose the snake to rattle his opponent. The snake would then crush a beer keg and get pie-eyed, which always brought a howl from spectators. Some say that Dixon kept the snake to scare off burglars and bill collectors. Others claim the snake eventually slithered from a winter snow and devoured Dixon.

"Maybe you better watch where you step," warned Alexis over the two way.

"That's not funny," said Jeremy marching forward while peeking backward, "How much farther to the munitions dump?"

"Looks like another 100 yards," replied Alexis with an eye on the GPS and a finger on the *talk* button. She picked an ice cube from a nearby water glass, and re-studied data supplied by Timothy J. Harper. The munitions dump would come first, followed by a small foot bridge and then the cabin. Pre-warned the hobo, *The area could be over grown with foliage since I last saw it.*

"There it is!" exclaimed Jeremy crossing the icy creek while shading weary eyes from the setting sun, "Dam, there it is."

The cabin stood like the vigilante, himself. An eerie silhouette in the setting sun. A grainy photograph taken with a box camera. Giant tree limbs shadowed broken timber logs. Two front windows looked like dark holes in a head skull.

"Sometimes it helps to whistle," suggested Alexis Grumman enjoying the moment.

"Do I sense a wise streak here?" asked Jeremy Wade tapping a solid front door while keeping Alexis on the line.

The door opened on a heavier series of raps.

All was dark inside.

Jeremy shone a flashlight, about.

No one was there.

"There's no one here," said Jeremy, breathing again while looking around.

"Lucky you," said Alexis, "So what do we have?"

A dirty egg skillet on a wood stove, and some fresh fireplace embers, collaborated the snowy footprints outside the cabin. Jeremy checked drawers in the one room lodging, and sorted through trousers hung in a metal closet. Tee's and socks were stuffed into a foot locker behind a lumpy cot. Said Jeremy, "Most of the garb here resembles that worn by the vigilante."

"Well, that explains the mystery of that yester-year look," said Alexis, "Now we need to find Jesse Joe Jacks."

Before they would find Jesse Joe Jacks, the vigilante found them. Jeremy stood just short of the creek bridge when Alexis texted-in over the two-way.

You have company,

Jeremy turned slowly.

The vigilante emerged from the shadowy trees.

Jeremy froze.

The vigilante stood feet spread, gun hand hanging below the Jordan holster strapped to his left leg. His flat brim hat tilted slightly. His dark-eyed stare locked in on the junior agent. The sought after star glistened from his cowboy vest.

"Oh shit," said Jeremy.

Show him your badge, texted Alexis.

Gingerly, Jeremy opened a leather wallet and produced an ID card.

"You're on private property," said the vigilante ignoring the identification.

"I'm a federal agent," replied Jeremy.

Jeremy, where's your badge?

With my street clothes

What the hell are you wearing?

A snow suit.

"You were in my cabin,"   said the vigilante.

"You're under arrest, Sir,"   said Jeremy.

"You were in my foot locker," said the vigilante.

Jeremy, read him his rights.

The junior agent tapped his two-way and brought up Miranda data supplied by Alexis Grumman. Said Jeremy reading aloud, "You have the right to remain silent . .Sir . .Anything you do or say can and will be held against you in a court of law."

Jeremy.

Yes Ma'am?

Scratch the part that allows him to terminate this interview at any time. That phrase is for here in Virginia.

Yes, Ma'am.

"You got five minutes to get off my land,"   said the vigilante.

Continued Jeremy reading aloud, "You have the right to an attorney. If you cannot afford an attorney, the court will appoint one for you, should your case go to trial."

Jeremy.

Yes, Ma'am?

Scratch that last reading. I forgot you are in New

Jersey. That part should read: We have no way of giving you a lawyer, but one will be appointed for you, if you wish, if and when you go to court.

"Scratch that last part," said Jeremy to the vigilante, "Let's start over."

"Time's up," said the vigilante to Jeremy.

"Jacks !" screamed Alexis Grumman going from text to speaker phone, "This is Lieutenant General Alexis Grumman from F.I.C. Headquarters. Stand down, soldier. I say again, stand down ! "

T'was a clever move by Alexis to defuse the situation, but an effort failed. A gun jumped into the vigilante's hand. Two shots rang out. The cartridges blew away the draw strings on each side of Jeremy's yellow snow pants.

The baggy trousers fell.

Jeremy's hand held device hit the ground with the lens pointed upward. The video camera began to run.

"Jeremy!" cried Alexis as the naked image came up on the big screen, "Where the hell is your under wear?"

As modesty would have it, Jeremy's two-way picked that precarious moment to die, and the wall screen went blank.

Befuddled, Jeremy pulled up the bottom half of his snow suit. He retrieved the fallen communicator and looked around.

The vigilante was gone.

CHAPTER 16

Special Agent, Joshua Joyner stood at parade rest before Lt General Alexis Grumman. Joyner wore jeans and a flannel shirt. His engineer boots needed polish, his crew cut reshaping.

Joyner came out of Quantico Marine Corps Base near Triangle, Virginia. He served brig time for a beer garden fight, before Martin Swan signed him up for The Invisible Six team. Josh held a black belt in Karate, and had two duty tours in Iraq to his credit. He took a crash course in espionage, and was now second in command under Colonel Martin Swan.

"I understand the Swans are in Paris?" asked Joyner who once shared a hayride with the current Mrs Swan.

"The Swans are in Cape Town," replied Alexis, "It seems Martin has international enemies. The FIC changed their European tour to a 30 day cruise below the equator, and what we say in this room, stays in this room. I think that goes without saying, and I assume you're short on shoe polish?"

"I'm incognito, Ma'am."

"That's bullshit, trooper," snapped the head of Paranormal Activities, "I want those boots shined and I want that hair cut."

"Yes, Ma'am,"

"Who's next?"

Zachery Roberts looked around the inner DPA conference room. Invisible Six members lounged on black leather seats positioned to face the giant wall screen. Alexis Grumman stood room center, clutching a long pointer designed for *show and tell* seminars. Jeremy Wade sat on a swivel chair with his foot cast propped across a computer desk. The projector man named Doug remained invisible. No one seemed inclined to move.

Slowly, Roberts took the floor.

"And I suppose you're a marine?" asked Alexis.

"No, Ma'am."

Swan recruited sniper Zachery Roberts from the United States Army. Roberts had an MOS of 111, and 112 which is light weapons and heavy weapons. The army has three categories for riflemen: marksman; sharp shooter and expect. Roberts fired expert with all weapons from all distances.

"And what exactly is it you do?" asked Alexis.

"Mostly Ma'am, I shoot pool and wrestle alligators," said Florida native, Zachery Roberts.

Laughter broke out.

Alexis Grumman smacked the pointer over Jeremy's foot cast, which dropped two pigeons with one pellet. The noisy room fell silent – and - Jeremy removed his autographed leg from the desk top, in a hurried move that toppled the shredder can.

"I'm sure Juan will enjoy picking paper dots out of the carpet," scolded Alexis referring to a day shift janitor. She then said to the group, "Who's next ?"

"Jocko Harrison," said agent James Harrison coming to parade rest, "Demolition rigger. If some--thing needs to be blown to bits, I'm your man. Large or small, makes no matter to me. I could probably plant a bomb in your cell phone."

"That's very comforting," muttered Alexis Grumman, "Next."

The last two squad members were Keith Jamison and Richard Kramer. Jamison doubled as motor pool mechanic, driver and heavy weapons. Kramer was a pilot. The sixth member of Martin Swan's infamous six was communication expect, Alvin Donner, who went down in a rain of gunfire at Black Water Crossing.

"The Invisible Six," whistled Jeremy Wade, "I

can't believe I'm sitting in the same room with the Invisible Six. You guys are a legend!! Trading gunfire with Colombian drug lords. Blowing up bridges. Chasing down the Taliban. Could you recount the assault on Mount St Helens for me? That's really my all time, favorite adventure tale."

Just about everyone over forty remembers the 1980 eruption of the Washington State volcano. The catastrophic event killed 57 people and destroyed 185 miles of roadway, including 250 homes and 47 bridges. It also spawned evil ideas among mindless men. The story goes that after 911, a small terrorist band dreamed of re staging the Mt St Helens eruption. The plan was to ignite the lava by dropping a bomb into the crater. All went well until the men parked at Windy Ridge where they discovered the bomb was too heavy to tote to the summit..

"That's when they decided to leave the bomb behind and backpack it upward with dynamite,"   said Josh Joyner.

"Dynamite?"   queried Alexis.

"We got this tip from a returning tourist at the visitors center,"   said Jocko Harrison,   "Actually, when we got to the summit, we found the climbers were only armed with fire crackers."

Alexis Grumman stared at Harrison. She stared at Josh Joyner who looked away quickly to hold a stolid face. Alexis popped a candy mint and chewed morosely on an ice cube before saying, "Doug, run everything we got on the vigilante. Pause at face closeups and quick draws. We have a situation here, Gentlemen. ..

. .and this is for real."

They sat for an hour and watched security tapes. Six men and one woman. As the films played out, the Invisible Six grew more solemn. Noise subsided, chuckles faded. The latest vigilante escapade even brought a outburst from sniper, Zachery Roberts who growled, "That sonofabitch hits what he aims at, without aiming."

The last security tape showed a bank robbery gone sour. Law enforcement had chased the thieves into a center city car wash. As the holdup car reached the tunnel exit, there stood the vigilante. The driver blew the horn and flashed his lights. Before police backup could reach the rear of the noisy tin building, the vigilante shot out the car lights, and flattened the two front tires.

"It's called point shooting," explained Alexis, smugly passing on learned information from a hand book by Bobby Lucky McDaniel, "The shooter uses a pointed finger and the mind's eye for a sight picture. The key is to shoot ahead and behind your target until the subconscious finds the middle. It does take practice. Many trainees begin with colored BB's which act as tracer bullets. BB's move slow enough to be picked up by the naked eye."

Savoring the moment to laud it over The Invisible Six, Alexis added, "I'm sure that *point shooting* would be a piece of cake for you gentle men."

"If my gun instructor caught me firing from the hip," grunted pilot, Richard Kramer, "He'd kick my butt."

"Ditto," chimed in Keith Jamison who specialized in howitzers and tank warfare.

"It looks like Hollywood to me," said squad leader, Josh Joyner.

"This is not tricked out film," said Alexis replying to whispers from the floor. Then after considerable pause she said, "I'm going to be upfront with you gentlemen. The deputy director wants your squad reinstated. He's willing to drop the misconduct charges incurred from the Black Water Crossing incident. . .namely. . feeding a live person to a live alligator. I'm not in agreement with FIC Director Taylor.

I want you gentlemen to know that. Unfortunately, I'm out ranked."

"What did forensics find at the cabin?" asked Josh Joyner, itchy to move the subject matter on.

"Mostly fingerprints," said Alexis.

"How about DNA?" asked agent Kramer, "Today's forensics can pretty much make a positive identification."

Alexis called for Doug to bring up a fresh set of images. She then tapped various black and white markings on the giant screen as she said, "We have no way to match up skin shavings and bite marks with a man who died fifty years ago. We did verify that the garb worn by the vigilante did at one time belong to Elk County game warden, Jesse Joe Jacks."

"And he died fifty years ago," reiterated Joyner.

"He died fifty years ago," verified Alexis.

"Any idea where this vigilante might go now?" asked Josh Joyner.

"That question is why you men are here," replied the DPA director, "Your mission is to first find this vigilante, then bring him in alive at all costs. We don't want this man dead. He's what we call a person of interest, I only hope you gentlemen are as good as you're bragged up to be."

CHAPTER 17

The vigilante struck twice more over the next three days, despite The Invisible Six regrouping. Alexis Grumman grew more frustrated. Vigilante tips fizzled. Authentic Jesse Joe Jacks fingerprints continued to trickle in. Media hype dominated the Six-0-Clock News.

"We got a call from Carson City police," said Alexis addressing the group, "Our vigilante gunned down five boys who raped and murdered a teenage girl near a freight yard, A witness claims the attackers were urinating on the dead body when a shot rang out. One boy fell, blood squirting from his mouth. All laughing ceased. A second shot sounded. A second boy went down. The third boy caught a bullet behind the head. The fourth boy threw up his hands to surrender. The vigilante shot him between the eyes, then gunned down the fifth boy on the dead run."

"This is definitely not a nice person," said Zachery Roberts who had more gun stock notches than cross ties on a railroad, "We could have used this guy in Kabul."

Infantryman, Jesse Joe Jacks saw his share of gunfire during the Korean War, a conflict that President

Harry S. Truman at first called a *police action.* Jacks fought at Osan, Pyongtaek, Chonan and Chochiwon, before being wounded at The Battle Of Taejeon. Jacks recovered to help allied forces push the KPA (Korean Peoples Army) from Pusan to Pyongyang, north of the 38 Parallel. Jacks came home with the purple heart and a footlocker full of medals.

"The man is more than a war hero," said Alexis, "He's what we call a survivor, and bringing him in could get bloody. Do we have the cabin sealed off?"

"Twenty four, seven" reassured Joyner.

"He must have an operations base elsewhere," ' said the DPA director.

"Maybe the street people are hiding him," said Josh Joyner.

"That's been suggested," said Alexis. "County authorities have sporadically checked out the homeless as best they can."

"Sporadically?" whistled Josh Joyner.

"Mt Loyal Mayor, Edward Morrison puts the county homeless figure somewhere around one thousand," said Alexis Grumman, who went on to elaborate on the leg work involved to cover the three municipalities that constitute Lower Elk County. Then watching Joyner check and double check his connection to Martin Swan, she asked, "You're worried about the Swans?"

"I can't seem to contact the Colonel," said Squad leader Josh Joyner.

"The Swans are in Nha Trang heading for Kuala Lumpur," explained the DPA director, "The cruise ship is holding up because of a possible typhoon at sea. And this is ironic. We have Colonel Swan out of communication range for his own safety, and now he's at the mercy of Mother Nature."

"Ironic indeed," agreed Josh Joyner.

"Anything else, agent?"

"Yes Ma'am," said the squad team leader, "Have you ever hunkered down in a snowsuit atop a mountain?"

"No, agent I haven't," replied Alexis.

"You'll be warmer if you take off your under wear," explained Josh Joyner winking at Jeremy Wade.

Alexis Grumman stifled a slight smile. She had the faceless Doug pull up GPS maps of Carson City, Hobbs Creek and Mount Loyal. Using the pointer she said, "Josh, I want you to take the team and recheck all homeless locations for these three municipalities. Half way houses. Missions. Railroad trestles. Dumpsters. Many cities now have what they call a *community coalition* to feed and shower street people. This gunman has to be somewhere and we have to find him."

"Alive," said Josh Joyner to the team.

"Thank you agent," said Alexis Grumman, "Any other questions, group?"

"I have a question," said Jeremy Wade.

"Yes, Agent Wade."

"How wide spread is that video clip of my testicles and the fallen snow suit?"

"I'm innocent," said Alexis.

"Stanley showed it to me," said Harrison.

"Stanley?" cried Jeremy, "What the hell's Stanley doing with it ! "

"It's on his cell phone," said agent Roberts.

"I saw it on You Tube," said agent Kramer.

"I understand it's coming to a cinema near you," said Josh Joyner.

CHAPTER 18

The vigilante mystery took an upward turn one week before Christmas. Hobbs Creek Police Chief, Adam Quayle sat staring at an idle ceiling fan when the phone rang. He listened intently, replaced the black plastic receiver and leaned back in the squeaky swivel chair that came with the territory. His brow wrinkled to a frown. He summoned the front desk via intercom, "Isabel, I need a duty log print out. . . make it for the last three weeks."

"Sorry Suh," replied the radio dispatcher, "I clocked out three minutes ago."

"Then have Potts do it."

"Sorry Suh, Mister Jeeter hasn't come in yet."

Adam Quayle groaned. Jeeter Potts had wife problems again, and was probably down at Fishers Pond, hurling snowballs at imaginary divorce lawyers. To make matters worst, Potts inadvertently held material pertaining to the vigilante case.

"Isabel, what is Jeeter's password?" asked Adam Quayle while poking keys on Potts' desktop computer,

"Can't give that out, Suh. "

"Isabel ! cried Adam Quayle, "I'm the chief of police !"

"Sorry Suh," said Isabel, "But I promised Mister Jeeter that nobody gets into his computer, and when I make a promise, I keep a promise."

"Meaning?" asked Quayle.

"Meaning I don't renege on my word," said Hobbs Creek's newest dispatcher.

"And I do?"

"You do," said Isabel.

"Isabel, is this about Monster Trucks?"

"It is."

"That was last March for chris'sake," said Adam Quayle, "And I never promised you the week off to attend the Silver Bowl. I promised to try and coincide your vacation with The Monster Jam World Finals. Unfortunately, Jeeter fell into Fishers Pond that week, and came down with pneumonia."

"Don't be blaming Mister Jeeter," said Isabel, "And I want you should know that's the first Jam I've missed in 14 years, including the Grateful Dead."

"Isabel, the Grateful Dead is a singing group."

"And the Silver Bowl is now Sam Boyd Stadium," retorted Isabel.

"Located in Whitney, Nevada," said Adam

Quayle.

"On East Russell Road," said Isabel.

"Hosts college bowls," said Adam Quayle.

"Also hosts local football games," said Isabel.

"Broke ground in 1970," countered Quayle.

"Originally named Las Vegas Stadium," said Isabel.

"Three and a half million to build," said Quayle

"Artificial Turf," said Isabel.

Adam Quayle quit the verbal ping pong match and went into networking on his own desk top computer. He traced out a few links without success. Quayle was not a computer geek and held no desire to become one. The seventy-something knew just enough cyberspace to get the job done, and wanted to keep it that way. He heard the station door close, and then reopen.

"What is it you need?" called in Isabel.

"Jeeter's dossier on the vigilante," called out Adam Quayle.

Moments later, Hobbs Creek's first black dispatcher filled Quayle's office doorway. She carried a giant handbag over one shoulder, and clutched a tattered scrapbook against her bulging uniform. She dropped the scrapbook on Quayle's desk, checked her watch and buttoned her ankle length, over coat. She cocked one ear toward Adam Quayle as she said,

"These are the newspaper clippings that Mister Jeeter saved from The City Press. The information here matches what he has in the computer."

"Thank you, Ms Jackson," said Quayle, "Change of heart?"

"Sometimes you're okay for a white boy," replied the off duty dispatcher with a wink and a smile.

Isabel Jackson was the former Isabel Brown who suffered a hearing loss while working for an upstate port authority. It was one of those *wrong place at the wrong time* things. As Isabel collected bridge fare, a wrinkled lady with a large bugle blew out her right ear drum. It was the first of three mishaps to befall Isabel in a year's time. Her daughter got knocked up by a white boy, and her husband ran off with the boy's mother, to audition for Dancing With The Stars.

Things brightened the following year. Isabel met Boa Beans Jackson, who was a Lower Elk County lawyer. Beans wasn't much interested in chasing down the Mr Brown, but his bespectacled eyes sparkled upon hearing the words, *port authority.* He took the libel case and gave a wedding band to Isabel, who relocated in

Hobbs Creek to qualify for a part time dispatcher opening. *To work here, you must live here,* Adam Quayle had said during their first encounter. A second interview bogged down over money and benefits. One month later, Mayor Willard Green III put Isabel on the day shift due to night blindness.

"So how's the case going?" asked Quayle.

"Which one," said Isabel, "The bridge people or the runaway spouse."

Smiling, Adam Quayle said, "I'm concerned about covering shifts. Should the bridge authority give you a million dollar settlement, I'll need to find another dispatcher."

"I'll give you two weeks notice before I leave," said Isabel peering over bifocals, "And Mister Jeeter keeps that scrapbook in the bottom desk drawer."

"I'll make sure it gets back," promised the Hobbs Creek Police Chief.

"Goodnight, Suh."

"Goodnight, Isabel."

Adam Quayle had newspaper clippings spread everywhere, as Jeeter Potts slipped into the station house through the back door. Said Quayle, "Nice you could make it."

"Sorry Chief," said the planet's oldest jitterbug, "Just be thankful you never married."

"Ah, the good life," replied Adam Quayle who often worked overtime, in lieu of going home to no one but a cat named Boots.

Quayle and Potts were cookie cutter images of the odd couple. Both lawmen took civil service exams at age eighteen, and joined the force shortly thereafter. However, similarities ended there. Quayle made rank quickly, Potts didn't. Quayle failed to find Mrs. Right. Potts found three. Quayle enjoyed fine wine, art and the theater. Potts drank cheap beer, watched cowboy movies and owned but one dress suit, bought from the church thrift store. Somehow, the two men became friends, and Quayle would sometimes eat at Jeeter's house for the holidays.

"This vigilante must have caught your fancy," said Quayle spreading the last clippings over plush carpet.

"The vigilante has caught everybody's fancy," said Jeeter Potts, "Are they my newspaper items?"

"Don't blame Isabel for giving up your scrap book," said Adam Quayle, "I pushed her into it."

Jeeter Potts dropped to the rug and began sorting the recent newspaper clippings that had yet to be arranged by time and date. Asked Potts, "What are we looking for?"

"We're looking for the vigilante," said Quayle.

"I don't think we are going to find the vigilante in these newspaper clippings," said Jeeter.

"Maybe we will," murmured the police chief sorting out more time and dates, "We need to put a name to this vigilante, He has to be somebody. He has to pay taxes. He has to have a drivers license. He has to live somewhere."

"He lived in his cabin," replied Jeeter Potts, "We know his clothes came from that dusty cedar closet. His fingerprints covered counter tops. He knew about the star. Who else would know about the badge and the significance of the badge. There's nothing here to investigate. "

"Maybe," said Adam Quayle.

"Chief, we both know this vigilante is Jacks," cried Jeeter tapping a photo on the desk top. "Be hanged what the feds think. We were here. We know what Jesse looked like. We know how he walked, how he carried himself. We saw him shoot. Jesse Joe is the only person who could be the vigilante."

"Jeeter," said Qualye, "Jesse Joe Jacks is dead."

"What if he's not?"

"In that case," said Quayle, "He would have gray hair and glasses, not to mention hearing aids and prostate trouble."

"What if this is one of those unexplained eerie things," suggested Jeeter Potts, "Like UFO's and lake monsters and the mystery of what happened to Uncle Horace."

"Uncle Horace?"

"My Uncle Horace."

"I didn't know you had an Uncle Horace," said Adam Quayle.

"On my mother's side," replied Jeeter, "Uncle Horace invented a car that would run on water."

"I thought that was a guy named Stanley," said Adam Quayle.

"My uncle's middle name was Stanley," said Jeeter Potts, "It was probably just coincidence. . .anyway. .one day he showed up missing."

"He showed up missing?" asked Quayle.

"Big as life," verified Jeeter Potts.

"Maybe the oil companies took him for a ride," said Adam Quayle.

"That's what we all figured," said Jeeter Potts, "The authorities found his car at a gas refinery, but we never found Uncle Horace."

QUANTUM ROOTS

Jeeter Potts came from a long line of inventors. His grandfather invented the submarine that wouldn't sink. His Uncle Henry invented a lead pencil with an eraser at each end. Explained Jeeter, "It was great for students who could not spell."

"Now I suppose you're gonna tell me it came with a lifetime guarantee," said Quayle.

"I don't know," said Jeeter Potts, "But it saved the system a lot of money on pencil sharpeners."

Adam Quayle waved a white hanky and finished surveying news paper clippings. He plopped back into the swivel chair. He spun to a side desk computer and hit the print function. He asked, "When was the last time Olan Chapman showed up for cards?"

"Week before Thanksgiving," replied Potts

"You seem pretty sure of that."

"Should be," laughed Jeeter, "I haven't won a game since he's been gone."

"Don't you find that strange?"

"There's nothing strange about it," said Jeeter, "Everybody knows Olan is the team. The man's got micro chips for a brain."

"I didn't mean card strange," said Quayle, "I meant strange that he hasn't showed up. "

"He has been a coma victim," reminded Jeeter Potts, "He'll be back."

"But he does love his cards," said Quayle.

"He does."

"And you two are friends?"

"We are," replied Jeeter Potts.

"Is Olan Chapman suicidal ?"

"You know I can't go there, Chief."

"Could Chapman suffer from a dissociative identity disorder?" asked Quayle.

"Split personality?"

"The same," verified the police chief.

Jeeter Potts walked to the window that over looked Main and Elm, just as the siren sounded across the busy street. He stood and watched a fire truck chase an ambulance into the noisy traffic. He returned to sit on the desk edge, arms crossed, feet dangling inches from the plush jade carpet. He said thoughtfully,

"I'm not sure where you are going with this, but Olan Chapman once led an anti gun rally in Hyde Park N.Y. He's very vocal against the N.R.A. Also, he was very supportive toward our local *Turn Your Gun In* program."

"That was the anti arms drive we ran a couple years back," recalled Adam Quayle.

"We didn't know Olan very well at that time," said Jeeter Potts.

"Maybe we still don't," said Quayle.

"Meaning?"

"I got a call earlier from Doc Belvins," said Quayle, "Ivy Chapman has made six appointments in three weeks for her husband. According to Belvins, Olan hasn't kept one. He comes home and disappears. Also, according to Belvins speaking for Mrs Chapman, Olin now calls his wife *ma'am* and won't sleep with her,"

"Chief, I wouldn't sleep with her, either," said Jeeter Potts, "She's got hairy forearms and a heart tattoo with an arrow through it. She looks like a dock worker. That tattoo belongs on a tree."

A wireless printer across the room finished spitting out paper. Quayle motioned to Potts who scooped up the scattered sheets.

"That's a printout of Isabel's duty log for the last month," said Adam Quayle, "I've had Ivy call me every time Olan shows up so Baker can serve this court order. Now, let's compare dates and call times against your newspaper clippings."

Moments went by. Eventually, Jeeter Potts looked up from the data and said, "Damn."

"Yes," agreed Adam Quayle, "Damn."

The facts were indisputable. Whenever Olan Chapman disappeared, the vigilante showed up, When the vigilante went idle, Olan Chapman was home.

CHAPTER 19

Ivy Chapman finished dishes and was folding clothes when the Invisible Six burst into her cabin. Calm turned to chaos, tranquility into trauma. They kicked through both doors, climbed over icy window sills. They barked commands, and held weapons in ready mode.

"What the hell are they doing!" screamed Alexis via Jeremy Wade's AV transmitter, receiver.

"They're not used to stateside missions," said Jeremy who possessed the entire Invisible Six data bank, "It was just a year ago they tied that Iraqi to his own pipe bomb. Found that guy's body parts all over Miami."

"Jeremy, I'm going to get my ass chewed out for this one !" cried Alexis.

"Here's more bad news," said Jeremy filming area events for FIC Headquarters via satellite, "There's a mob forming out front."

Maryann Grundy lived next door to the Chap mans. They were not coffee clutch, but Maryann was block captain and head of the neighbor hood watch program. She was appointed to that position by peers who vacationed in Lake Powhatan, then returned to city life. Maryann, who was a single mother, stayed put. Thus, she was the best candidate for the job. Also, Maryann had roots here. She was daughter to Tom and Angel Grundy who originally owned Cabin 20 back in the fifties. Upon her parents death, Maryann inherited the lakefront dwelling, when her twin sister moved to San Diego.

At times, Maryann became vigilante minded. Earlier, she spotted six dark figures circling the Chapman cabin. Instead of calling police, she notified her first lieutenant who made the first two pyramid calls. Each of those recipients then called two more people who called two more people, etc etc. Fifty odd residents now stood in front of Cabin Eighteen. One man held a bull horn.

"Jeremy, who the hell is this?" said Alexis Grumman via the two way.

"His name is Horatio," replied Jeremy Wade, "He's the voice for the CFA."

"What the hell is the CFA?"

"Citizens For Action," said Jeremy, "This is another group inspired by the vigilante."

"YOU INSIDE !" blared the bullhorn, "LET THE LADY GO ! TAKE ME AS HOSTAGE, INSTEAD

"Horatio, I'm already outside," said Ivy.

"Stand clear, Ma'am," said the CFA spokesman, "I'm experienced in these hostage situations."

"But Horatio -

"YOU INSIDE !" blared the bullhorn, "LET THE LADY GO AND NOBODY GETS HURT !"

"Horatio -

"Please Ma'am, I'm negotiating."

"LAST CHANCE DIRT BAGS," blared the bullhorn, " IF I HAVE TO COME IN THERE, I WILL KICK SOME BUTT !"

Ivy Chapman reached forward and tapped the CFA spokesman on the shoulder. Said Ivy , "Horatio, I'm right here behind you. I'm trying to talk to Chief Quayle. Could you turn that thing off a minute."

"Ivy, you are upset," said Adam Quayle from the desk phone at police headquarters.

"Adam !" cried Ivy Chapman into a cell phone, "I've got six armed men in my cabin running room to room, waving guns and yelling *clear.*"

"Ivy, they are just securing the building," explained the Hobbs Creek police chief.

"Securing the building? Adam, this is a four room cabin for chris'sake. They're scaring the shit out of the rabbits. I've got two broken windows and a busted door latch. I can't find my freaking husband who won't sleep with me and calls me ma'am. Animal control is waiting down the block with somebody from the board of health. And you think I'm upset. I'm not upset, Adam. I'm pissed off !"

"Jeremy," said Alexis via satellite, "Instruct Joyner to circle the men at parade rest outside the cabin. Nobody – and I mean nobody - is to enter. I'm bringing in forensics."

"What about Mrs Chapman?"

"Do what you do best," said the DPA director, "Sweet talk her."

Fingerprints taken from Cabin 18 at
Lake Powhatan were found to match those
of Jesse Joe Jacks, aka The Vigilante.

Part Three

CHAPTER 20

Darkness fell as Olan Chapman stepped from the bus onto an icy Hyde Park street. He was tired, cold and hungry. The trip from South Jersey to New York State had been a series of bus journeys, thumb rides and long walks. He paused to adjust a weighty backpack, then continued on until he reached a brown bungalow with an outside garage.

All lights were out, street traffic quiet. A backyard dog whimpered. Distant children waged a snowball fight just off the familiar banks of Gill Creek.

Chapman smiled. His once owned silver out board rested on two saw horses behind the garage. His used pickup sat in the driveway. Fortunately, the new owner kept the same key under the same floor mat.

Missing was the boat trailer

Chapman eased the battered white pickup from the driveway to the street. Two blocks later, he flicked on the headlights. Now, the *All Points Bulletin* fugitive needed to find a boat trailer and some food. He tackled the boat trailer issue first. An hour later he confiscated a rusty steel rig from a down town boat yard. However, the stolen trailer came with a problem. The steel ball mounted on the pickup was smaller than the hitch on the trailer. Thus, every road bump caused the trailer to jump loose from the truck. Chapman solved that issue by lashing the rig to the truck's undercarriage. He would abandon the trailer with an apology for the boat yard. Eventually, the authorities would find the truck, but the boat would never return. And that pricked his conscience.

Traffic thinned as he merged from Rt 62 into Packard Ave. He turned onto Veterans and parked when he reached the dead end at Buffalo Road. The Niagara River lie straight ahead. He would travel from this point on, using a canal that ran through a tank yard, and emptied into the dark waters that roared over the falls.

Next problem.

The bank slope was steep.

Very steep.

QUANTUM ROOTS

Chapman elected to leave the trailer road side, and hand-drag the outboard to the water. Sirens sounded close by. A freight train rumbled in the distance. Chapman paddled the boat where he could, waded where he couldn't. Panting, he pulled the boat along. Twice, he had to belly down to get under a low overpass. When he reached the Robert Moses Parkway, flashing lights overhead caused him to pull up short.

His feet were now numb, his arms weary.

Time seemed to stop.

The lights moved on.

Chapman dragged the outboard to a mid-way point beneath the overpass. A rusty ring protruded from a sagging timber. He anchored the boat to the ring. He paused to stare through the portal that showcased the Niagara River. The angry currents that rushed toward The Falls seemed immune to time and decay, milestones and misery,

He uprooted a sign that said no boating.

He made his way back to the truck.

*   *   *   *   *

"Come in brother," said a cheery sister framed in the mission doorway, "All are welcome here."

Dinner was long over, but bread and soup were still on tap. Olan Chapman sat on a rickety chair under a long table covered with crumbs and dried coffee stains. He was out of gas, out of money and still 40 miles from Buffalo city limits.

"How do you feel about cycles," said a bearded left over from the Sixties peace movement.

"Beats walking," replied a grateful Olan Chap man, "Not many people left who will pick up a hiker."

"You don't look very dangerous," growled the biker who dropped his passenger off with a well meant warning, "Watch your back here, stranger. Bad section of town if you know what I mean."

Olan Chapman disappeared behind a billboard, his satchel in hand. He returned wearing the black brim hat over his matted hair, and the tan ammo vest beneath his fur lined jacket. The 45 hung low on his left hip.

He turned on a cleated heel and walked toward the back streets of Buffalo City.

CHAPTER 21

December 21

Buffalo jumped with busy shoppers, crowded buses and pushy cab drivers. Christmas sights and sounds abounded from back alleys to city hall.

Arthur Kinney drove into an underground garage and parked in a reserved spot near the elevators. He pushed a dashboard button marked *power,* and a blue light went out as the electric motor powered down. He smiled at a buzzer that reminded him to take the keys. He plugged an orange charge cord into a nearby electrical box, and walked briskly to the elevators.

"You are loving your new car," said a sleepy secretary as he walked through a door marked KINNEY, LAMB and FOXX.

"It shows?" he asked .

"It shows," she replied while walking to a filing cabinet. Her name was Susanne Woods, her job description covered potpourri. She came to KINNEY, LAMB & FOXX as a mere girl, and knew where the bodies were buried. Face wrinkles now peeked through heavy makeup, but time had been kind to her leggy body.

"You know me too well," said the senior member of a three man lawyer team that chased ambulances and targeted insurance companies. Currently, the firm's case load ran light which brought overhead to the foreground. Something had to be done. They came up with a three part solution: cut TV ads; move to a lower rent district in Buffalo City; buy electric vehicles. Exclaimed Kinney, "Would you believe I came all the way in here on no gas."

"You have a guest waiting," said Susanne.

"That would be Tootsie Moore," said Arthur Kinney cleaning eye glasses with a business suit hanky. He patted down a trim mustache and rubbed palms together as he said, "She's the lady that got run over by a city school bus. We're going to make our rent this month."

"It's not Tootsie Moore," said Susanne, "Unless she's masquerading as a cowboy."

Kinney draped a wool scarf over a plastic hanger, and turned with overcoat in hand, to shoot Susan a questioning look.

"It's him," she replied, "He's back."

"I thought he relocated to Jersey," said Kinney, the happy face turning downward.

The secretary shrugged.

All three attorneys shared the same receptionist-secretary, but worked from separate rooms. Arthur Kinney's office was the first door on the left, down a short hall. He told Susanne to hold all calls and burst into his office saying, "Alright Olan, let's not start this shit up again."

The vigilante stood braced against an open window. He stared down at a back alley dumpster as a noisy trash truck approached. He turned to eyeball a water stained ceiling and a frayed floor rug. A torn lamp shade exposed a bare bulb. A water cooler sign read *out of order.* He said, "I'm glad to see you're not doing so well."

"Please close the window," said Arthur Kinney, "I'm not heating the great outdoors. . . and Olan. . . I'll draw up a fresh restraining order if I have to. You're not going to badger me. You're not going to bother my secretary. Also, I hope that gun you are wearing is a cap pistol. If not, you better have a permit to carry."

The phone rang.

"Susanne, I said to hold all calls."

"This one's important," replied the desk phone.

"I can wait," said the vigilante.

"Thank you," snapped Arthur Kinney.

Ms Elena Tootsie Moore wanted to drop the libel suit against the city transit company. Ms Moore now claimed her back pain disappeared after two aspirin and a hot bath. Ms Moore also stated that pretending injury where there was no injury, was illegal as well as immoral. Arthur Kinney then told Ms Moore that the doctor's examination confirmed two ruptured disks and a possible fractured tail bone. After which Ms Moore agreed to rethink the situation and call back.

"Olan, I'm sorry your sister got raped," said Kinney looking up from the phone call, "I'm sorry she died, but it's time to let it go. That was twenty years ago, Olan. We were juveniles, just kids."

"There were three of you," said the vigilante without turning from the window. He spoke louder to cancel trash truck sounds from below, "You, Zelly and Jarod, . . you held her arms. . .Zelly held her ankles. . .Jarod raped her.."

"Alan, let it go for gods'sake," pleaded the senior attorney for Kinney, Lamb & Kox, "You were told to let it go. My father told you to let it go. Dr Dearwood told you to let it go."

"Your father's as guilty as you are," said the steady voice of the vigilante.

QUANTUM ROOTS

"My father's dead, Olan."

"So is my sister."

"That was Jarod's doing," said Arthur Kinney, "She wouldn't stop screaming. Jarod grabbed her by the throat to keep her quiet. We didn't want her to die. It just happened."

The phone rang. It was Tootsie Moore. Her back felt wonderful. Her back felt better now in fact, than when she played left wing for the high school, hockey team . She was dropping the case. Her husband wanted her to drop the suit. Her kids wanted her to forget it. The local priest advised her to show up for Saturday confession. The thinking was over. She was dropping the case.

Kinney slammed down the receiver. He jumped from the desk and brushed by the vigilante en route to close the open window Tin cans rattled from below as he snarled, "Olan, it's time you found out the truth. Your sister was a cock teaser, okay. Those freaking mini skirts she wore. That fat ass she wiggled at every boy in school. Olan, your sister was a slut and far as I'm concerned, she got what was coming to her."

Susanne the secretary hung up on a sales call just as the gunshot sounded. The sharp crack echoed out into the empty hall. She covered her mouth as though to seal off a scream. She uncovered her mouth. She rose cautiously from her cushy chair as the vigilante emerged from the inner office. She froze as he walked by the reception desk. He stopped at the outer office door and drew his firearm. She shrank backward and prepared to take cover. The vigilante used the gun butt to smash out the window glass that read   KINNEY LAMB & FOXX.

"You're gonna need a new sign,"   he said.

Relief set in as apprehension mounted. The vigilante disappeared. Susan made the sign of the cross. She then went to investigate. Kinney's office was empty. Sounds of commotion filtered up from the street. She ran to the open window and peered down.

She gasped.

Arthur Kinney lay draped over the trash truck, below.

CHAPTER 22

Allison Zeller pulled into the driveway with the lights off. She almost raised the noisy garage door from force of habit. Quickly, Allison swapped the opener for the front door key. She killed the car engine and caught the time as the dashboard light went out.

It was 2am.

All was still.

She straightened her lipstick and made sure her bra and panties were on. She opened a gum stick to combat a whiskey smell and readied the door key.

She stole into the house.

"Damn you Sparky," she said tripping over the cat, who took off for parts unknown.

She was Benjamin Zeller's third wife. She was 15 years his junior and didn't dance to heavy metal music. She didn't like cats, abhorred house work and suffered dark nightmares over childbirth possibilities. She crept through the house, shoes in hand, eyes darting about.

Light shown from the basement stairs.

"Shit," said Allison stopping at the stair case. She put on her shoes, descended the bare wood steps and walked briskly toward the den area saying,   "Okay, so you are up."

Earlier, Allison went mall shopping with her childhood friend, Vicki Sue Jennings. The two girls had a history. They graduated from jump rope to white lace, together. Allison served as Maid Of Honor for Vicki Sue, and one year later, Vicki Sue returned the favor when Allison married the town banker, Benjamin Zeller.

Ironically, Allison was the prettier of the two girls, but somehow Vicki Sue lassoed the better husband. Howard Jennings nailed down a lucrative pharmaceutical job, gave Vicki Sue the proverbial white picket fence and two gifted children. It was a scenario custom made for Wheel Of Fortune. Mean while, Allison discovered Benjamin snored, clacked his false teeth constantly, and used low limit credit cards. He also possessed an ugly temper and scowled at any one under thirty.

Then Mister Right came along for Allison.

Roger Clydesdale was the golf pro at the country club where Howard Jennings married the former Vicki Sue Ryan. Somehow, Roger's lady-friend and Allison fought over the same bridal bouquet. Later, the two women became friends. Then, Allison and Roger became friends. Best friends. Roger gave Allison a few golf lessons with a nine iron, which led to more lessons with a driver. Afterward, they would have meaningful talks about money, cruises and the high cost of divorce. Now it was time to get honest with the score card. It was not fair to use Vicki Sue as an alibi any longer.

Allison took a deep breath and walked through the partition door to the basement den.

She stopped cold.

There was not going to be any fight.

Benjamin Zeller lay twisted over his get-a-away suitcases. Money and blood covered the vanilla rug. A toppled phone lay near the body. Sparky the cat showed up briefly, and quickly vanished.

Allison covered her eyes. She took a deep breath and uncovered her eyes. She stood frozen, memorized by the moment The toppled handset also lay dead silent, an indicator the receiver had been off awhile. Obviously, there had been no 911 call and no response. She hung up the phone and opened her cell.

"Roger?"

"Ally! I'm sorry about the toenails."

"Roger."

"Honestly Ally, I meant to have them cut."

"Roger!"

"Ally, what is it?"

Allison Zeller took one final look at the blood, the money and the body. Then she turned away saying, "Roger, you're not going to believe this shit."

Sometime earlier:

"I'm leaving this town," said Benjamin Z. Zeller throwing paper money into two full size suitcases, "I'd advise you do the same."

"Zelly, I'll take care of Chapman," reassured a raspy voice from the far end of the phone.

"Jarod, are you listening?" cried the center city banker, "This guy's a killer. He took out Artie with a single shot, then dumped his body out a three story window. Currently, he's a media folk hero. . and frankly, I don't think the cops want to catch this vigilante."

Bank Vice President, Benjamin Zeller lived in a stone mansion that overlooked the Niagara River. The thirty-nine year old was thrice married, twice divorced. He fathered one son by his second wife, named Sarah. The frail ten-year old boy lived with Zeller's first wife, Thelma Sue – for reasons only understood by soap box opera fans. Zeller's main concerns were turning forty, hair loss and the vigilante.

Now, Zeller sat on his carpeted basement floor, unloading a safe prepared for what Zeller forecast as a financial Armageddon. Ben Zeller was convinced that markets would soon crash, and folks would once more be selling apples on street corners. Little did this investment counselor ever imagine that the timid Olan Chapman would show up as his Waterloo.

"Maybe this guy isn't really Olan Chapman," suggested Jarod Purdy from the desk of his down town job site, "Could be just a look-a-like."

"Arthur's secretary identified the voice," said Zeller, "She also remembered this guy wore elevator shoe lifts and heel cleats. Chapman wears shoe lifts and heel cleats. They make him feel bigger than life."

"Chapman's not a gunfighter," argued the raspy phone voice, "He's a pussy. Besides, what makes you think this vigilante would be chasing us."

"I spoke with Susanne on the phone," replied Zeller, "Susanne is Arthur's secretary. And according to her, this vigilante made a threat going out the door. He said *one down, two to go.*"

Silence.

Continued Zeller, "And I would also advise you not to disappear using credit cards, bank cards or IP addresses. We both know Olan's a computer geek. The only thing he can't track is cold cash."

Breaking window glass disrupted the talk. Heel cleats descended the basement steps. Benjamin Zeller dropped the house phone. He pulled a 38 special from the safe. He spun and fired wildly at the silhouette outlined on the far wall. As fate dictated, he hit the stairway bulb and that portion of the basement went black. He emptied the police special into the darkness.

The vigilante fired once.

Benjamin Zeller briefly saw a flash and then slumped to the floor.

The vigilante stepped over the suitcases and picked up the squawking phone. He whispered into the receiver, "Zelly has nothing more to say."

"It is you," said the distant voice,

"You're next, Jarod."

"Olan, you little piss ant. I knew you were watching. I should have killed you then."

"You tried."

"I couldn't find you," said the distant voice.

"You can find me now," said the vigilante.

"Olan, you asshole," cried Jarod Purdy with a forced laugh, "You never shot anything in your worth--less life but a cap pistol and a potato gun."

Said the vigilante, "Give me a time and a place."

CHAPTER 23

Jeremy Wade hobbled up the concrete steps of the new FIC building, just off the Eastern By Pass. The vigilante had finally crossed state lines, and the F.I.C. was in full pursuit mode.

"I need to see your ID," said the security guard.

"Stanley, it's Christmas," said Jeremy.

"I'll call backup," threatened the guard.

"I hope Santa pees down your chimney," said Jeremy as he produced a photo card and submitted to a body scan, "What's the commotion out there on the highway?"

"Accident," said Stanley, "Head on. Some semi crossed the media strip."

"Looks like the same trailer," said Jeremy.

"It is," said Stanley, "Same spot, same driver, different tractor."

"She in?" asked Jeremy referring to Alexis.

"Of course she is," said the solemn guard, "That is why you are here."

"So the night does have a thousand eyes," said Jeremy who paused for an additional floor check and hand scan, before entering DPA head quarters. He paused again for ice water and a handful of pepper mints from a reception table.

"You're stealing the boss's candy," said a file clerk loaded down with paper trail documents, "I'm snitching."

"I'd like to steal her candy," murmured Jeremy as he entered the inner door.

The conference room buzzed with activity. White shirts and black ties milled around like so many cattle in a corral. Alexis Grumman and her expandable pointer stood room center. Said the female Lt General to Jeremy, "You are late."

"My foot bandage needed changing," said Jeremy Wade hopping onto a conference table shaped like a peanut.

"That's bullshit, agent," said Alexis, "And get your ass off the table top.

"Yes, Ma'am."

"We got a call from Buffalo City police," said Alexis addressing the group, "Our vigilante gunned down two unarmed men, yesterday. One victim was the vice president of a bank, the other a senior attorney for a law firm."

"Isn't that out of character for the vigilante?" asked a newly assigned agent.

"That was our first thought," said Alexis.

"What's the vigilante doing in Buffalo, New York?" asked an agent on loan from IC.

"And you are?" asked Alexis.

"Agent Spicer, on loan from CIA."

"The vigilante's from New York State, Spicer," replied Alexis, "Doug, bring up what we have on Chapman. Put the prints on split screen."

Olan Chapman was born to a William and Hildegard Chapman in Buffalo, NY on August 8, 1974. The boy grew up behind locked gates, and attended a private school. When he turned eight years old, he watched three high school boys rape and murder his older sister who attended a public school. Young Olan ran and hid. Two years later, the family relocated to the Hyde Park section of Niagara Falls. A prominent therapist prescribed the move to help young Olan forget the horrific event. Concluded Alexis, "Now here's the kicker. These latest victims were two of those three boys."

"Do we have names?" asked Agent Spicer.

"Arthur Kinney, Benjamin Zeller and Jarod Purdy," said Alexis, "The girl's name was Rebecca Ann

Chapman. There's no record of a trial in our 1982 archives, due to obvious factors. All persons involved were juveniles at the time., and the body disappeared."

"Convenient," said Agent Spicer, "No body, no case."

"Suspicions and conjecture ran rapid," said the DPA director, "Jarod Purdy had an uncle who owned a crematory. After a year of fruitless searches, rumor had it that Purdy's uncle disposed of the body. Officially, the case sits in the unsolved files."

"So, the vigilante really is Olan Chapman," said another newly assigned agent.

"It gets better," replied Alexis pointing toward the split screen, "These are the prints we lifted from Cabin Eighteen at Lake Powhatan. These prints belong to Olan Chapman. Now, we have two more prints. This next print belongs to the vigilante. We got this print from a shell casing at the airport. Our third print comes from Korean War archives. This print belongs to the county game warden named Jesse Joe Jacks, who died some fifty years ago. All three prints match."

"Ouch!" cried someone in the room.

"And here's more," said Alexis reading from a hand held, "We have case files for Olan Chapman and Jesse Joe Jacks. Both men have similar physical data.

Medium height. Slim. Caucasian with dark features. IQ's are within 2 points of each other. IQ's of course can fluctuate with age and drowsiness. Psychological profile runs almost parallel. Both men are characterized as being anti socials who wear elevated shoes. Jacks even wore cleats. We have an eye witness who claims the vigilante wore cleats. She remembers a metal tapping sound as the vigilante filled the doorway."

Alexis Grumman sipped more ice water and popped another candy mint. She glanced up from the hand held, "And now we get to one glaring difference. Medical files suggest Olan Chapman could be suicidal. Army records define Jesse Joe Jacks as mentally sound.

"What's the status on the third attacker?" asked an agent on loan from the FBI.

"The third alleged attacker is why we're here," said Alexis, "His name is Jarod Purdy. He sells used cars in Buffalo City. He's the last target standing, so to speak. He called us for federal protection. In return, he's agreed to help us set up the vigilante,

Alexis Grumman pointed at a river span on the giant wall screen and went on to say, "This is Rainbow Bridge at Niagara Falls. This bridge connects the USA with Canada. A pedestrian walkway runs along the west side. Jarod Purdy and the vigilante will have a showdown tomorrow on this walk way . . .set up of course by Mr. Purdy."

"At high noon?" asked a graying agent with a slight smile.

"Of course," replied Alexis without missing a beat, "Purdy will enter the bridge from our side. The vigilante will approach from the north. The two will meet at a name plate that reads *International Boundaries*."

"How will the vigilante get into Canada?" asked an unnamed agent.

"Purdy feels he's already there. Purdy believes the vigilante takes refuge across the border," replied Alexis, who then said over the intercom, "Doug, pan out on the aerial map of New York State."

Buffalo City, Niagara Falls and Hyde Park form a skinny triangle just south-east of the Canadian border. Alan Chapman grew up in that triangle. He would bicycle through Hyde Park, hike through Goat Island. In later years, he honey- mooned at Horseshoe Falls. He also sold cable boxes throughout Niagara County, while working his way up to computer programmer.

"Which means he's a leg up," said Alexis, "He knows where the cracks in the wall are."

"So where do we come in?" asked Spicer.

"I sent Swan's team north," said Alexis, "I need you men to set up a communication network between their assigned positions and this headquarters. We have a plan, but it's a bit tricky."

"Tricky," said Spicer "Tricky scares me."

"Anything that interfaces with the Invisible Six will likely scare you," said Alexis Grumman.

"I hope we're not going to shoot a live person out of a circus cannon," said Agent Spicer who worked with Martin Swan during Operation: *Big Top*.

"Actually, our plan satisfies American Civil Liberties Union requirements," said Alexis.

The fore mentioned, border plaque marks the midway point of Rainbow bridge. Two flags fly opposite the bronze marker. The Director's plan was to lure the vigilante inside Stars and Stripes territory, after which pilot Richard Kramer would swoop in from points unseen, and air-drop a giant net over the unsuspecting vigilante.

"You're shitting me," said Agent Spicer.

"*You're shitting me* is not an appropriate response for a federal agent, Spicer."

"Purdy agreed to decoy this operation?" asked a faceless agent from the group.

"The walkway is nine hundred and fifty foot

long," explained Alexis Grumman, "Purdy's job is too hang back until the vigilante steps into our jurisdiction. Then we drop the net. The operative slogan here is *bring 'em back alive.* And that's not a suggestion, gentlemen, That's an order. And it's an order from upstairs. You chase him down if need be. Tackle him. But, don't shoot him."

"Should I pack up my long johns?" asked Jeremy Wade.

"Negative," said Alexis Grumman, "You're not headed north, Jeremy. You're going to Paradise Island. You have a luncheon date Friday with a Dr Daly."

"Male or female?" asked Jeremy.

"Norman Daly is a retired physicist from Upton, New York," replied Alexis, "He wrote a book entitled Quantum Roots, which might explain how Olan Chapman and Jesse Joe Jacks could be the same person."

"Sounds like science fiction," said Spicer.

"Ditto," agreed Alexis Grumman, "Anyway, the good doctor has agreed to see us."

Are you going with me? texted Jeremy to the DPA director.

Negative, replied Alexis Grumman, *Put your dreams back in your pocket, Jeremy.*

CHAPTER 24

Next Day: High Noon.

Leroy Dobbs stood before a giant picture window and watched the vigilante kick tires on a four wheel drive, pickup truck. Dobbs squashed a fat cigar into a glass ashtray marked *Dobbs Car Sales*, and waddled outside to shake hands with what appeared to be a potential truck sale.

The vigilante stood with hands braced on the cab roof and peered at the truck's interior. He needed a shave and a bath. The flat brim stetson covered his matted hair. A long trench coat concealed the forty-five.

"This is your lucky day," said Leroy Dobbs, "You're our one millionth customer, which means I'm in a position to offer you the deal of your lifetime on this four wheel, anti-skid, four on the floor, with a souped-up jimmy engine, that will do zero to sixty in six seconds, heat and air included, tommy lift, rear window slide, and pay no mind to that puddle under the radiator. We had rain this morning and that just happens to be low ground."

"Jarod Purdy," said the vigilante.

"Oh."

"Is he here?"   asked the vigilante.

"He's out to lunch,"   replied Leroy Dobbs pointing toward a sales trailer stationed under a net work of bare light bulbs,   "You can wait for him in there. He'll be back in ten."

Jarod Purdy once owned a full fledged car dealership that catered to high-end clients in and around Buffalo City. Purdy employed a dozen salesmen, garage mechanics, three service managers and one very overworked janitor. Now, fresh out of prison for income tax evasion, Purdy sold cars under Leroy Dobbs' dealership license. The bottom line worked for Dobbs. When Purdy sold a vehicle, Dobbs got a cut of the action.

"Do me a favor?"   asked the vigilante.

"Name it,"   said Leroy Dobbs.

"Don't tell Jarod Purdy I'm here,"   said the vigilante,   "I want to surprise him."

"You got it."

Dobbs watched the vigilante disappear into Jarod's sales trailer. Dobbs then returned to his own desk. He was on the phone when Jarod Purdy slid a burger bag and some fries across the shabby linoleum floor.

"I hope you didn't get me onions," said Dobbs smelling the air, "I like them okay, they just don't like me. Especially, later on."

"No onions," replied Purdy, "Just a thank you for taking me on. Most dealerships won't give an ex-con the time of day."

Dobbs was back at the window to watch Purdy enter the sales trailer that overlooked the used car lot. He was about to turn away when the gunshot sounded. Seconds later, Purdy blew backward out the door and landed face up in the snow.

"You are supposed to be on Rainbow Bridge," said the vigilante standing over the body.

"I'll see you in hell," cried Jarod coughing up blood.

"Been there and back," said Jesse Joe Jacks who mowed down countless orientals in Korea – some warm, some frozen.

"Who the hell are you?" sobbed Jarod Purdy staring into the blurry face of the vigilante, "You're not Olan Chapman."

"What happened to the body?" asked the vigilante.

Rebecca Ann Chapman was raped and killed in a wooded grove behind a private school play ground. The high school junior was homeward bound from a late cheerleader practice. She was dragged to the ground by three teenage boys who went unpunished for lack of a body, coupled with political connections held by the Kinney family. After the assault, Jarod Purdy strangled the leggy cheerleader to keep her from talking. Olan Chapman was a lone eye-witness. A school janitor found the eight year old the next morning, huddled up in the basement boiler room.

"I knew he was watching," wheezed Purdy, "I wanted to kill him too, but I couldn't find the kid."

"What happened to the girl's body?"

"My uncle cremated it," said Purdy as his voice began to trail off. "No corpse, no case. . and for what it's worth . .whoever the hell you are. . . Chapman's sister was a little cock teaser. . .somebody should have told the kid that for gods-sake."

Jarod Purdy stopped spitting blood. His black eyes rolled upward. His head slumped back.

He died.

The vigilante stood over the still body. Methodically, he fired shot after shot into the silent corpse. With each bullet, the body would lurch. The vigilante then dropped the empty revolver into his waiting holster. He unpinned the tarnished star from his vest and dropped the tarnished badge onto the dead body.

He whispered, "Done."

"Oh shit," cried Leroy Dobbs coughing up hamburger covered with ketchup. He bolted the front door shut for fear that death was headed his way. He stumbled to the desk and groped for the phone. His voice shook as he called 911.

"Oh shit is not considered an emergency," said the operator, "Try to remain calm and tell me what happened,"

"What happened ?" cried LeRoy Dobbs, "How the hell do I know what happened ! Maybe somebody was not happy with their car."

Several relay calls later, Lieutenant General Alexis Grumman pushed the *end call* button back at DPA headquarters. She looked at Jeremy Wade and said, "We've been snookered."

"Snookered?" said Jeremy with a smile.

"Bamboozled," said Alexis who went on to outline the car lot shooting, "Nobody showed up at Rainbow Bridge but us."

"So that's it," said the junior agent, "It's over."

"Not yet," replied Alexis Grumman, "We still have to catch the vigilante."

PART   FOUR

CHAPTER 25

Franky and Jonny were sweethearts, but not the Frankie and Johnny of song lyrics. Franky was Francine Alberta Morton of Northeast Philly, who graduated with honors from Penn University, and now waited tables at a Frankford Ave diner. The dark haired beauty enjoyed shopping, travel and playing hide and seek with a pet gerbil named Harry. Jonny was Jo Ann Wilson who dropped out of grade school to become a garage mechanic. Her life now centered around hair nets and heavy layers of fingernail polish.

The two girls met while fighting over a parking spot at weight watchers. It was love at first sight. Jo Ann hollered bitch at Francine who called Jo Ann a whore, After which, the two girls kissed and eloped to Las Vegas, Nevada. Now, they stood in a Philadelphia travel agency to carry out a conventional honey moon.

"We're making a statement here," said Jo Ann Wilson, "We're coming out of the closet."

"I think that's already been done," said a busy desk clerk with a phone in one ear, "Maybe you could try a bomber jacket and a tattoo."

"Yes," bubbled the blue eyed blonde, "I like that. I like that !"

"I thought you might," said the busy clerk running their credit card, "If you're crossing the Rainbow Bridge, you'll need a visa,"

"We are not going to any Canada," exclaimed Francine, "Brand names are pricy enough here ."

The busy desk clerk hung up the phone and opened a fresh travel brochure. Our Lady Of Fatima in Youngstown, NY was currently running dazzling light displays for Christmas. Visitors could also see the Avenue Of Saints from atop the Basilica. The clerk's proposed tour would fly the two girls from Philadelphia International to Niagara International in time for the 15 acre religious display.

The following morning, the female newly weds would bus to Goat Island, and then hike to an area called Top Of The Falls.

"Awesome !" cried Jo Ann Wilson.

"What !" screamed Francine Morton.

"Do I smell a problem here?" asked the clerk checking brochure against computer data.

"Who dreamed up this crap!" demanded Francine, "Goat Island ?"

The clerk closed the folder and peered over reading glasses at the blonde who turned to the brunette and cried, "Francine, we are trying to make a statement, here."

"Screw the statement," replied Francine, "I'm going shopping and I'm not stepping over bear shit to buy a new wardrobe."

"Bears don't inhabit Goat Island," said the clerk as a point of fact.

"Whatever," said Francine heading out.

The clerk quickly opened another brochure. Buffalo, also known as the "Queen City", offers many winter attractions and mucho year around shopping. An inner section named Elmwood Village runs a *tour by foot* to countless boutiques and gift shops with something for everyone. And for those with an open itinerary, One Walden Galleria awaits. The double level mall contains two hundred stores, ten restaurants, an international food court and the Regal Cinema 16, that shows the latest and greatest on the big screen.

"Now you are talking," said Francine returning to a rickety bar stool positioned between Jo Ann Wilson and the booking counter, "And you need to know I'm not opposed to suing anybody, anytime at any place."

"Maybe you should remain standing," said the counter clerk.

"Franky !" cried Jo Ann, "We're not here to shop. Women shop. We're here to brave the elements. Witness the icy Falls. Cruise on the Maid Of The Mist."

The Maid Of The Mist water cruise is a featured attraction at this Western New York State, tourist center. The double deck vessel leaves a Canadian dock at Clifton Hill, and journeys to Horseshoe Basin where rain coated tourists greet the Falls, up close and personal. Hours vary depending on weather and holidays, making it best to call ahead.

"The Maid Of The Mist is closed until May," said the travel clerk.

"Then we'll visit the windy cave," said Jo Ann.

"I think you mean Cave Of The Winds?"

"Yes," said Jo Ann, "Cave Of The Winds."

"That's closed, too."

Cave Of The Winds was originally a natural cave behind Bridal Veil Falls. Rockfalls and dynamite slowly obliterated the cave in 1954. Today, sightseers can stand on redwood decks at the Falls baseline, and experience the awesome roar of crashing water. After which, they ride an elevator back to the top ground.

"Park officials remove the observation decking this time of year," said the counter clerk, "Potential ice can damage the wood."

"This is not going well," said Jo Ann Wilson talking over street horns coming through the front door, "Can we start over?"

"Of course," said the clerk.

"A man and a woman get married,"

"Of course."

"They honeymoon at Niagara Falls."

"I'm with you."

"They view the Falls from a cruise ship called Maid Of The Mist."

"Keep going."

"Now, Franky and I get married," continued Jo Ann, "But we're both female."

"Yes, I've noticed."

"We honeymoon at Niagara Falls and we cruise on a ship called Maid Of The Mist."

"Wrong," said the clerk.

"Wrong?"

"The cruise is closed for the winter."

"But the Falls is still operational?"

"Yes."

"I think we are being discriminated against," said Jo Ann wrinkling her tiny nose, "Can we start over?'

"Of course," said the clerk, "How about we start with a different credit card. This one appears to be all stocked up."

"Franky, give her your credit card."

"No."

"No?"

"Jo Ann, I'm not gonna track through snow to some place called Goat Island. I don't even like goats."

"There are no goats on Goat Island," said the counter clerk who went on to explain that Goat Island was dubbed Goat Island in the late seventeen hundreds. A pioneer named John Stedman kept a herd of goats on the wooded tract that divides Horseshoe Falls from Bridal Veil Falls. Icy weather forced Stedman to vacate the island in the severe winter of 1780. He returned later to find all the goats had died but one - hence the name, Goat Island.

"That's so interesting !" bubbled Jo Ann Wilson, "I read somewhere that 40 million gallons of water go over the Falls every minute, and that the average temperature inside the windy cave is 55 degrees, Fahrenheit."

"Cave Of The Winds," corrected the clerk.

"Do I look like I give a shit?" asked Francine Morton.

"Franky!" cried Jo Ann, "I think you have lost sight of our mission. We have a chance here to take a giant step for women-kind everywhere."

"I'm here to buy a pants suit," said Francine.

"I never realized you are so materialistic," said Jo Ann

"Im also buying shoes," continued Francine.

"What happened to *getting in touch with our inner feelings*?" asked Jo Ann.

"I'm very much in touch with myself," said Francine Morton, "And right now my inner feelings tell me I want a new pants suit and some new oxfords. I always feel better when I get new shoes. Maybe brown this time, with white toes. I'll have to pick out the suit first, of course."

"I'm getting pissed, Franky."

"Better cover your ears," said Francine looking at the counter clerk, "And hold onto to that paper weight. She also throws things, like frying pans."

"At least I know how to cook," snorted Jo Ann.

"You two don't seem to be on the same page," noted the counter clerk.

"I would say the same cook book," said Jo Ann, "Maybe we need a trial separation."

"Fine," spit the masculine looking Francine, "We'll throw in the towel. But at the price of gold today, I want my ring back."

"Oh !" screamed Jo Ann Wilson stamping her feet on linoleum tiles made to look like wood, "You are impossible. What did I ever see in you !"

"It's probably the size of her dildo," suggested the counter clerk.

"How do you know about my dildo?" asked Francine.

"I might have the answer for you two girls" said the counter clerk pulling more trip tickets from a display cabinet. She then proceeded to give Francine a shopping tour through Buffalo, and Jo Ann a bus ticket to Goat Island.

Thus, it would come to pass that the bubble headed blonde from Northeast Philly, would count among those few, who experienced a verbal encounter with a dead man,

named Jesse Joe Jacks.

CHAPTER 26

Goat Island plays a key role for those who would witness the awesome thunder generated by Niagara Falls. This uninhibited land tract contains a lookout post named Terrapin Point, where tourists can see The American Falls, Bridal Veil Falls and Canadian Horseshoe Falls, collectively called Niagara Falls. To stand on the Point is to literally hover over the Falls, as this noisy cliff splits the international waters into the three separate Falls.

Visitors also have access to an observation tower, and can purchase tickets for the waterfall cruise, Cave Of The Winds and Journey Behind The Falls.

Two bridges bring tourists onto the island. A narrow foot bridge accommodates pedestrians, a wider bridge serves car and trackless trains. This resort area offers three gift shops and a restaurant. A visitor center welcomes all on a year round basis. The island contains two reservations and endless foot trails that lead everywhere. A winding two-lane avenue called Goat Island Road encircles the entire woodsy area.

QUANTUM ROOTS

Team leader, Josh Joyner deployed the Invisible Six at various points around the island perimeter. He stationed himself at the welcome center on downtown Prospect Street, to halt tour groups that would enter Goat Island.

Earlier, an anonymous caller had phoned in a vigilante sighting on Goat Island..

The call first came into Hobbs Creek dispatch. Isabel Jackson then told Adam Quayle who called Jeremy Wade, who texted Alexis Grumman, who assigned a video camera to each hand gun, and a tripod to every look out tower along the Niagara River.

Joyner now stood on the blue entrance steps to the giant glass building that advertised food, gifts and sights. He stared up at the vertical orange signs as he texted on his two-way.

General, if one of your film jockeys gets in the line of fire, I'll shoot the sonofabitch." .

You're such a joy to work with, agent Joyner.

You sound like Colonel Swan. . .why would the call come in to Hobbs Creek?

We don't know, agent. Did I hear a toilet flush?

I was in the food court when we lost phone contact, texted Joyner.

I hope we're gonna run this mission sometime, today, texted back Alexis.

Yes Sir, as soon as we secure the area, replied the Invisible Six team leader.

What's the holdup Joyner and I'm not a sir.

The Tours R Tours, Christmas Tour was the hold up. A small french lady with a large bullhorn counted heads. Earlier, she entered the island over the Pedestrian Bridge, trailed by ten yellow parkas, who would brave icy elements to witness the Falls in winter. She intended to exit the island with ten yellow parkas. Satisfied every one was accounted for, she barked out a command and marched off into wind driven snow.

"Delta One, this is Delta Two" said a reconnaissance agent over the squad's private band, "Tour group has left the island."

"Roger that," replied Joyner, "Close the net."

Quietly, The Invisible Six snaked toward the island's center. Sniper Zachery Roberts and demolition rigger, Jimmy James Harrison moved in from Terrapin Point. Cannon Ball, Keith Jamison bellied in from Three Sisters Island. Pilot Richard Kramer and the new communications man crept in from an empty parking lot at the island's south end. Joyner ditched his unmarked car at First Avenue and Goat Island Road, then zigzag-ed on by foot. Kramer had suggested choppers to search and capture, but Joyner feared any aerial maneuver might spook the subject.

Snowy ground made the *crouch and run* a long haul. Icy winds didn't help. Methodically, the Invisible Six moved toward the co ordinates that matched those of this latest vigilante sighting. Finally, the call came in to Josh Joyner.

"Delta One, this is Delta Four, over."

"This is Delta One, come back."

"We got him."

The familiar black stetson and long leather blazer sat on a park bench near the island's mid-point. Hands were tied, mouth gagged. The Invisible Six approached with weapons pointed upward. As they circled the wrought iron bench, they quickly lowered their 9mm's so each gun barrel pointed toward the target's head. Joyner reached down and yanked away the black stetson.

An ocean of blond hair tumbled out.

"Damn," cried Joyner pulling out his two-way as a camera jockey moved in, "Command Center, we need the EMS unit out here, pronto. This girl's half frozen !"

CHAPTER 27

Niagara Falls treatment centers host a revolving door policy. Hours run twenty-four, seven. Cases are varied. Jumpers can suddenly show up on the brink of the Falls, regardless of weather. Barrel enthusiasts occasionally ignore the Niagara Parks Act and challenge the Falls to find a spot in the sun. Some survive, others perish.

In 1859, stuntman Jean Francois Gravelet crossed the gorge on a tight rope. In 1901, Annie Edison Taylor went over the Falls in the first recorded barrel incident. Guess work claims some 5000 bodies have washed over the edge since 1850 – many intentional. Bottom line: thrill seekers are drawn to the Falls like climbers to a mountain.

Frostbite is common over winter months.

Alexis Grumman stood bedside pulling clutter from a giant, basket weave handbag. She found her laminated ID as she spoke, "I'm Lieutenant General Grumman and I need to ask you a few questions."

JoAnn Wilson rolled face down and fist-pounded the motorized mattress. She was now thawed out and fear turned to anger, because Francine Morton had yet to contact the hospital concerning Jo Ann's condition. Also, Jo Ann's roommate was a fat man with a nose wart, who would not shut up. The fat man was also a frostbite victim. Park guards managed to grab the man just before he went over the Falls in a giant rubber ducky.

"It's not easy being fat with a nose wart," said the fat man, "On July 4, 1928, Jean Lussier went over the falls in a large rubber ball, and he made headlines."

"Just a few questions," said Alexis Grumman peering from fat man to girl, "Then I'm outta here."

"I can't believe she hasn't called," cried Jo Ann.

"Who's she?' asked Alexis.

"My significant other," replied Jo Ann Wilson, "Francine Morton from Northeast Philly.

"You're married to a woman?" asked Alexis Grumman.

"We're trying to make a statement here," said Jo Ann, "The whole world needs to know that two women can marry and honeymoon at Niagara Falls, just like any other couple."

"Hasn't that already been done?" asked Alexis.

"I'm so hurt," said Jo Ann.

"Timi Yuro," said a bed pan nurse entering the

room, "1961. Her birth name was Rosemary."

"I'll never fall in love again," said Jo Ann.

"Tom Jones," said the nurse exiting the room, "I love Tom Jones with all that chest hair ."

"Just a couple questions?" asked Alexis.

"I'm just too depressed for questions right now," said Jo Ann Wilson, "One really is the loneliest number."

"There's room in my rubber ducky for two," said the fat man, "It might seem dangerous, but you won't die for lack of air."

On July 4, 1930, George Stathakis went over the falls in a barrel, He became stuck behind a water curtain for 18 hours, where he suffocated from lack of oxygen.

"But he did survive the initial fall," pointed out the fat man.

"I'm happy for him," said Jo Ann.

More challenges for Niagara Falls waited down the road. On August 5, 1951, William "Red" Hill, Jr. went over the falls in a vessel named *The Thing*. The homemade craft broke apart on bottom rocks and Hill was killed. 1961 – On July 15, William Fitzgerald went over the falls in a rubber ball nicknamed the *Plunge-O-Sphere*. On July 3, 1984 Karel Soucek went over the falls in a barrel. His rate of descent was clocked out at

75mph. Soucek suffered minor injuries, only. One year later, a Steve Trotter went over the falls successfully in a barrel. Concluded the fat man, "On June 18, 1995, Trotter went over the falls again successfully with a Ms Lori Martin."

Jo Ann suddenly stopped sobbing and snapped at the fat man, "I am not going over the Falls with you in a rubber ducky !"

"Can we get back on track here," said Alexis closing a curtain between the two beds. Then talking to Jo Ann, she asked, "What can you tell me about the vigilante?"

"My favorite story is the cat who went over the Falls in a barrel," bubbled the fat man from behind the curtain.

"I don't know any vigilante," said Jo Ann answering the DPA director.

"The man who swapped clothes with you," explained Alexis, "We need to find him."

"Oh, the guy with the little penis," said Jo Ann.

"How do you know he has a little penis," exclaimed Alexis, "Did he try and molest you?"

A rotund black nurse entered the recovery room to take blood pressure readings. She pulled an intravenous tube from Jo Ann Wilson's arm, and stated that the doctor was late making rounds. Chuckling, she added, "When the weather turns this frigid, every man has a tiny penis. Even my man."

"That's true," said the fat man from behind the white draw curtain, "And sometimes I can't even find my penis."

"Nurse," said Alexis Grumman, "When did hospital rooms go co-ed?"

"We're out of beds honey," said the nurse, "Besides, frostbites are mostly out-patients."

Alexis turned to Jo Ann and asked, "Do you have a cell phone?"

"That man took it," replied Jo Ann, "Then he left me there to die."

"He didn't leave you there to die," said Alexis, "He used your yellow parka to melt in with the tour group. He then used your phone to give us your location."

Alexis Grumman turned on a heel and walked to the nurses aid station. A busy uniform paused to study the federal ID, and then put Alexis in touch with hospital administration. Moments later, Alexis hung up the counter phone and returned to Jo Ann Wilson. Said Alexis, "You're being moved to a single room. Before I go, I need that phone number. It's not coming up under

Jo Ann Wilson."

"It's under Morton," sobbed Jo Ann rolling her head back under the pillow.

"Of course," murmured Alexis heading for coffee and some window glass that would enable her two-way to text, "Why didn't I think of that."

Jeremy. The vigilante has a phone. Jo Ann Wilson's phone. And that gives us a number for satellite tracking. However, I'm not sure who is chasing whom. Once the vigilante took the victim's phone, he could have called 911 to rescue the girl. He didn't. Instead, he called Hobbs Creek, knowing they would contact us. Jesse Joe Jacks couldn't do that. He wouldn't know how to operate a cell phone. But, Olan Chapman would.

Now for the flip side.

The caller used the phonetic alphabet to give the girl's location – this according to Isabel Jackson. He used George, Oboe, Able and Tare to spell Goat Island. Those words are from the Army phonetic alphabet used during the Korean War, Chapman wouldn't know that, but Jacks would.

Bottom line, Jeremy.

It's now more important than ever, that you make that plane for Paradise Island - Alexis

CHAPTER 28

Agents Josh Joyner and Reuben Goldberg sped past two pole flags on the Rainbow Bridge, that divide the United States from Canada. They slid over icy road conditions into customs. Joyner flashed an ID badge at a somber lady wearing a red-orange emblem on a uniform shirt. Agent Goldberg dug out a debit card from a heavy overcoat.

"I need to see a passport," said the border agent.

"What happened to *Welcome To Canada?*" asked Josh Joyner.

"If you don't have a passport," said the sober agent, "A birth certificate or drivers license will work."

"I'm federal," said Josh Joyner.

"I'm tired," said the border agent, "Where's your picture on this ID?"

"I'm a number," explained Joyner.

The border guard typed data from both ID cards into a keyboard, mounted inside her window booth. She handed the cards back, saying, "I see your partner has a photo ID."

"New man," explained Joyner, "He hasn't become invisible yet,"

"He might want to lose some weight first," said the border guard.

"Have you had that hair bun long?" asked Joyner, "I thought they went out with penny candy."

"I think I'll have your car searched for alcohol and tobacco," said the border agent.

Alexis, we might need some help here, texted Joyner as he pulled away from customs.

To be sure.

Flashing lights and angry sirens filled the Ontario air as Josh Joyner jumped the media strip at Newman Hill and took Falls Avenue west. Border patrol cars zeroed in from all directions. Joyner handed an ID card to the inquiring officer, and mentioned professional courtesy.

Alexis, we need some help here.

Moments later, Joyner and Reuben Goldberg were on the road again. Border patrol cars trailed behind until Joyner passed the Hard Rock Cafe. Then, the red and blue flashes disappeared as the two U.S. federal agents melted into the Niagara Parkway.

"The CBSA stands for the Canadian Border Service Agency," explained Reuben Goldberg referring to letters on the border patrol cars, "And let me take this moment to say what a great honor this is for me. I can't believe I'm working with the Invisible Six."

Alexis, who is this guy?"

Reuben Goldberg, texted back the DPA Director, *I brought him up from headquarters to replace Donner.*

Alexis, this guy has a pot belly.

He's up to date on the Global Intelligence Grid, Joyner. And , he understands Net-Centric Warfare.

"Sir, It's not safe to text while you drive," said Agent Goldberg, "And I think you have over looked your seat belt."

Alexis, this guy could be a counter spy.

Reuben Goldberg wasn't a double agent. The twenty-five-year old Mensa, graduated from Colorado Technical University at Colorado Springs, where he majored in tel-communications. After which, he attended Boston U for post graduate work. FIC picked him up peeling potatoes and walking guard duty at Fort McNair, D.C.

"The Army was my best bet," explained Reuben Goldberg who failed to find work in the post 2008 job market, "I don't fly, and ocean waves upset my biological balance."

Alexis, did the colonel approve this kid ?

Joyner, this little wild bunch show that you and Colonel Swan run, is coming to a close. The department aims to replace the Invisible Six with responsible, knowledgeable agents. Trust me, Colonel Swan will be notified when he and the child bride come up for air. And Joyner. . . federal agents do not tell Canadian customs to blow it out their ass. . .and. . .you don't address me as Alexis.

Yes Sir . ..I mean Ma'am.

I'm happy to see we are making headway.

Jo Ann Wilson's cell phone showed up a few miles down the road. Her yellow parka lay folded near a sprinkler head hidden by snow. The phone sat on the parka. Agent Joyner braked across the highway in a double loop that parks tourist buses. He dodged the Niagara Parkway traffic and returned with the soggy parka, and one really damp keypad.

"That's why we kept losing the signal," explained the junior agent who stayed with the car, because running always made him winded, "Wet circuits will do it every time."

"Yes they will," said Josh Joyner who stepped outside the olive drab car to look around. Niagara Falls thundered to the south. The Skylon Observation Tower loomed to the northeast. Multi- destination buses filled the two parking loops. Joyner flipped open his two-way and said, "We got the parka, General. We got the phone. We don't got the vigilante."

"Search the buses," replied Alexis.

"No point in closing the barn door now," said Josh Joyner.

"We have a description update," said Alexis, "Search the buses."

Earlier, two daylight robberies took place in down town Niagara City. A man clad in a yellow parka waltzed out of a clothing store wearing black denims, a black stetson and a bright red, snow jacket. He carried the yellow parka under one arm, according to unidentified witnesses. Shortly thereafter, a red and black clad male robbed a center city sporting goods store. In the second burglary, the hunting store owner said the armed bandit made off with 45 caliber blanks. Local authorities believe both robberies point to the vigilante.

"General, we have no jurisdiction over here to search or seize buses," said Josh Joyner.

"I'll clear it through channels and keep an eye on Reuben," said Alexis Grumman, "He's not fond of firearms."

QUANTUM ROOTS

"Ducky," growled Josh Joyner heading toward the first bus in line, "I wonder why the vigilante would steal a bright red jacket and a box of blanks?"

"Catch him and we will ask him," replied Alexis Grumman.

CHAPTER 29

The jumbo jet dropped through blowing rain and bounced onto the Nassau International run way. Once inside the Lynden Pindling terminal, Jeremy Wade found the rendezvous sign that read Baggage Weight Allowances.

"Nasty weather out there," said the special agent shaking hands with Dr. Norman Arnold Daly, "I'm Agent Jeremy Wade."

"I go by *Hey Doc* mostly," said the retired physicist staring downward, "That cast must be very uncomfortable."

"I was fighting the bad guys," said Jeremy, "Missed with a judo kick and dented a steel pole. My doctor claims I cracked a talus bone, whatever that is. I think it has something to do with the ankle."

"I had the same misfortune a while back," said the physicist/science writer from Upton, NY, "Only I fractured my ankle stumbling into a pot hole."

The two men ducked into the airport bar to wait out the rare winter rainstorm. The physicist ordered whiskey on the rocks. Jeremy checked his two-way and ordered soda. A cold beer would come later. Meanwhile, he was still on duty.

"Commendable," acknowledged Dr. Daly.

"I need a run down on your book," said Jeremy

"Which one?" asked Daly

"There's more than one?"

"I have two published books on the market," said the well known scientist, "Golden Stream and Quantum Roots. Golden Stream is my best seller. The book suggests that creation forms from streams of energy. I published it under my pen name, I.P. Daly."

"I'm here to talk about Quantum Roots," said Jeremy Wade.

"Of course," said Norman Daly, "I've been contacted by the Federal Intelligence Center. Someone named Alexis Grumman mentioned a paranormal event. She said you might have a question or two."

"I have a problem," said Jeremy.

"Don't we all," said Daly, quickly downing a second shot on the rocks.

Continued Jeremy Wade, "We have a man born in 1923, who died in 1959. We have a second man born in 1973 who is currently in hiding. Both men came from different parents. Both men share the same fingerprints."

"You do have a problem," said Norman Daly waving off a third drink. Then he faced Jeremy to ask, "Do you like fish?"

"Love fish," replied the junior agent.

"Good," said Daly.

The two men drove through busy downtown Nassau and parked in the sandy lot of a fish fry. They sat on an upper deck and watched rain patter off distant picnic tables. Sudden wind gusts lifted a loose umbrella, and sent the yellow shade cover sailing into some nearby palm trees. Dr Norman Daly opened a copy of his book titled *Quantum Roots*, and pointed to an illustration that resembled a giant turbine. Said Daly,

"This is a picture of the LHC (Large Hadron Collider). Man-made fury you might say. This energy collider, and earlier particle smashers have greatly changed the way we see time, space and matter."

"Meaning?" queried Jeremy Wade.

"Time and space are not a framework that creation attaches itself to - like we once thought. Rather, energy forms the time and space when sub atomic particles explode from a quantum state to a physical state. The particles have been there all along. Thus, time and space are merely byproducts of energy."

"Is this goodbye to the Big Bang?" asked Jeremy.

"On the contrary," replied Daly, "Every form of creation from the flea to the universe, begins with a genetic explosion. Whether it's big or not is relative. And, it's not a beginning. It's just a point in a cycle."

Jeremy, are you drinking a beer?

I'm eating lobster and corn fritters, Alexis..

I think you're drinking a beer, Jeremy.

"Your wife?" inquired Daly sneaking a peek at the agent's classified communicator.

"My boss," said Jeremy.

"Lucky man," said Norman Daly

Get back to the book, Jeremy.

"My book is geared toward space travel," explained the noted physicist talking to both Jeremy and his two-way, "Conventional space travel sends a man to the moon, and his root configuration follows. My quest is to transfer his genetic blueprint to a point in space, and the man will follow."

"Is this like connect the dots and you come up with a picture?" asked Jeremy.

"It's more like connect the quarks," said Daly, "It's the quarks that define a person. My peers ran an interesting experiment back in 2004. They collapsed some quarks to a micro hole. They shot the hole with ionized rays from gold bars to excite the quarks, which in turn exploded, and emerged from the hole back in their original form. We believe this happens because quarks retain their properties,

"Bear in mind that every piece of particle energy formats with a given genetic frequency that I call a quantum root. My plan is to collapse quarks to a black hole. Next, we establish a frequency generator on a distant planet such as Gliese 581d. We then produce the genetic frequencies that format with the collapsed quarks. And presto, the quarks seek their roots immediately. Space travel in a flash."

Jeremy, get away from this kook-a-boo."

Alexis, there was a time when the two-way, wrist radio was far fetched.

Jeremy, this guy has a black mustache and a orange goatee and why is that girl at the next table giving you the big eye?

You're jealous.

I'm not jealous and stop trying to cover up the video screen.

"Now, back to your fingerprint dilemma," said the noted physicist, "We don't physically come from our parents. We actually come through our parents.

However, the odds of two different couples producing the same genetic code in this universe, would be like catching lightning in a bottle. For starters, the human gene count has been revised from 30,000 to 50,000 upward. Now, add in the 3.1 million energy bits that format with each gene, and you get the scope of the problem."

"How about multiple universes?" inquired Jeremy.

"I'm not sure I believe in a universe," said Norman Daly, "It could be we live in some kind of *wave* field where *forces* interface with recycled energy. There might be a point in this field where all particle energy collapses, which would result in one colossal Big Bang. Or, it might be that existence relies on nature's balance. Where as, too much particle energy collapses to a quantum state, and an overload of quantum energy explodes to a particle realm. Or, it could be there's a universe for every grain of sand."

Jeremy, get away from this kook-a-boo !

A dark skinned man with fat lips and white apron set a cold beer on the canvass table cover. A gold tooth flashed as he pushed the drink toward Jeremy and said,

"Compliments from the mademoiselle at the bar, suh."

Jeremy, I have a cab waiting for you downstairs. Now!

"I have to go," said Jeremy shaking hands with the noted physicist, "Duty calls."

"You like this Alexis," flatly said Norman Daly.

"You're very perceptive," replied Jeremy Wade, "Frankly, I'd swim through five miles of jelly fish, just to smell her panties go by in a rowboat."

Norman Daly laughed and said, "Now that's what I call selective breeding. . .and Jeremy, for Jacks and Chapman to be the same person, Jacks needed to die totally and completely. He had to leave this world almost in a flash."

The special agent paused at the wood banister that led downstairs. He gave the waiting taxi a high sign. He turned to lock eyes with the noted physicist and said, "He did."

CHAPTER 30

He ran through the briars and he ran through the brambles, and he ran through the bushes where the rabbits couldn't go. He ran so fast that the hounds couldn't catch him, from Mississippi banks to the Gulf Of Mexico.

"Joyner, we have gunshots coming from Hyde Park," screamed Alexis Grumman over the two-way, back at DPA headquarters, "Witnesses claim shooter is firing at a paper target pinned to a giant oak tree. Exact location unknown. Shooter description: Caucasian male dressed in red parka and black stetson. !"

"How the hell did he get back in the States," replied Josh Joyner, "I thought customs was notified."

"What's your ten-twenty, Joyner?"

"I'm still at the bus depot on Niagara Parkway."

"Where's Agent Goldberg?" demanded Alexis.

"Agent Goldberg is ten-one hundred," replied Josh Joyner staring at the awesome waterfall across the river.

"What the hell is ten-one hundred, Joyner?"

"Agent Goldberg is taking a piss," replied the squad leader for the Invisible Six, "Agent Goldberg claims that the Falls makes his bladder run."

"Joyner, he better not be behind a bush."

"One of the buses has a toilet, General."

F.I.C. Headquarters housed two helicopters on the reinforced rooftop of the three story building. The modified UH60 Black Hawks were fondly nicknamed, Barracuda One and Barracuda Two. They were equipped with M60 machine guns, missile launchers, longbow radar and the latest military computer systems for combat operations. The two *super sonic* choppers now sat in the west side parking lot on Goat Island. Agents Zachery Roberts, Jocko Harrison, Keith Jamison and Richard Kramer stood by.

"Roberts, you and Harrison canvass north of Porter Road," instructed Alexis, "Kramer, you take Jamison and search south of Porter Road. Joyner and Goldberg will patrol Hyde Boulevard."

"Excuse me, General," said Josh Joyner.

"What is it Joyner?"

"This is still Colonel Swan's unit," said the squad leader, "And this unit goes by the chain of command. . .with all respect, General."

"I stand corrected," said Alexis Grumman.

Agent Reuben Goldberg returned from the bus stop. As he climbed into the passenger seat, Joyner said to Alexis, "General, I don't team up Zach with Jocko for a reason. Last time I did that, they tossed a terrorist out of an airplane."

"That was not a good thing," said Agent Goldberg joining the conversation.

"From thirty thousand feet," remembered James Jocko Harrison breaking radio silence.

"No," said Goldberg.

"Yes," said Harrison.

"Parachute?" asked Goldberg

"No parachute," replied Harrison.

"He must have been terrified," said Reuben Goldberg, innocently.

"Not as frightened as the four diplomats in the limousine," said agent Zachery Roberts.

"I don't have any data on four diplomats in a limousine," said Alexis Grumman over the two-way.

The falling terrorist caved in the car top of a conference limousine en route to Geneva. Two Middle East ambassadors were killed instantly, two died in a Scotland hospital.

"No," said Reuben Goldberg.

"Yes," said Josh Joyner.

"That must have been the main topic at the conference table," said Goldberg.

"Peace bead sales took a beating," said agent Zackery Roberts

"Agent Joyner?" broke in Alexis.

"Yes, General?"

"Can we proceed with this mission?"

"Yes Ma'am," replied Joyner, "We need to patrol the Gill Creek waterway that flows through Hyde Park and empties into the Niagara River." .

Proceed soldier, texted back Alexis.

Minutes later, two choppers flew over the Hyde Park section of Niagara City. The park has few trees and much open area which makes aerial surveillance an easy chore. Agents Kramer and Roberts hovered over the tennis courts, picnic areas, and Sal Maglio Stadium. Agents Harrison and Jamison patrolled up and down Gill Creek. Team leader Josh Joyner and rookie agent, Reuben Goldberg pulled into the open field just south of Porter Road.

"Sir, I think we're exceeding the speed limit," said Reuben Goldberg.

Josh Joyner braked under a giant shade tree that over looked the open field. He pulled a white poster board from the tree trunk. A painted bulls eye had been shot out. He said into the two-way, "No sign of any other target, General."

"Why does a wanted man fire a gun in an open field," asked Alexis from DPA headquarters, "The whole park is surrounded by homes. He has to know some one will call it in."

"I don't know," said Josh Joyner, "Maybe he wants us to chase him."

*   *   *   *   *

Comes Olan Chapman. Two hands on one oar. Black hat brim tilted low. Gliding quietly over still waters. A fleeting silhouette, all but hidden from human eye by roadside shrubbery and tall grasses. When he reached Walnut Avenue and Hyde Park Boulevard, he dragged the weathered canoe through the busy intersection and disappeared over the far side bank.

"I've got a bead on him !" cried agent Jocko Harrison over the two-way, "He just hand-carried the canoe across Niagara Street. You can pick him up where Gill Creek passes under Packard Road."

"Roger that," confirmed Josh Joyner from behind the wheel of the government issue sedan. He stopped canvassing the general area and took Royal Avenue to Packard Road. He parked in an empty lot that overlooked Gill Creek. The Packard overpass lay to his left. Across the street, the Gill Park footbridge spanned the narrow creek waters. He put away his communication device and loaded his 9mm.

"It's time for me to swing into action," said Reuben Goldberg.

"Time for you to swing into action?" echoed Joyner.

"Such a dream come true," bubbled the team's newest squad member, "Me, Reuben Goldberg. A member of the Invisible Six. My little brother Lenny will be green with envy."

"Josh, we want this vigilante alive," said Alexis over the two-way as Agent Goldberg left the car, and headed across Hyde Park Boulavard.

"I don't think we have much to worry about," replied Joyner as Goldberg tripped over the street curb.

Silver cage fence surrounded the walkway bridge that crossed Gill Creek. Reuben Goldberg crawled over a concrete cistern cover and began to climb over the gate. A large lady with a small dog approached.

"Sir, that's a no no," said the fat lady.

"I'm a federal agent," replied Goldberg.

"And I'm Cinderella," said the fat lady.

QUANTUM ROOTS

"Seriously," said Reuben Goldberg, "I'm one of the Invisible Six."

"You might think about losing some weight," said the fat lady.

"I'm on a mission here" said Goldberg.

"You don't look like a federal agent."

"Ma'am, your dog is biting my leg."

"Poopsie doesn't like you," said the fat lady who recently returned home from a Florida vacation. She pulled a 911 phone from her handbag and said, "I hope you have some ID."

Olan Chapman paddled within view, some one-hundred feet up stream. Reuben Goldberg fell over the gate top and bounced off the decking. He picked up his mega horn and ran to the bridge center. He pointed his 9mm over the railing. Chapman stopped paddling. Goldberg sat the 9mm down and picked up the mega horn.

"Mr Vigilante, this is Agent Goldberg."

No answer.

"I don't want to hurt you," boomed agent Goldberg over the mega horn, "Pull your canoe off to the side of the creek!"

No answer.

"Mr Vigilante, this is your last chance !"

No answer.

Reuben Goldberg sat the mega horn down and picked up the 9mm. Chapman sat the oar down and picked up a three foot section of heavy duty, plastic pipe. He stuffed a potato down one end. He shot aerosol spray in the opposite end, and quickly replaced a breach cover. He placed his trigger finger on a lever that ignited a spark plug.

Reuben Goldberg pointed his 9mm handgun at his target.

Chapman pointed the pipe barrel at Reuben.

"Last chance!" hollered Reuben.

Chapman pulled the lever.

Witnesses would later claim that the *BOOM* echoed from Buffalo, New York to Toronto, Ontario. One elderly gentleman swears the roar blew off his hearing aid. Another report claimed the noise dwarfed that of Niagara Falls.

"What the hell was that!" cried Josh Joyner.

"That was a potato gun," replied agent Keith Jamison from the copter overhead.

The potato caught Reuben Goldberg in the chest. Sheer force sent the rookie agent staggering backward across the bridge, where he toppled over the rail and splashed into Gill Creek. The fat lady picked up the small dog and scurried off. Her fallen phone continued to talk by the wayside.

"Where the hell did he get a potato gun," cried Josh Joyner.

"Same place he got the canoe," replied Alexis from DPA Headquarters, "We have an update here, gentlemen. The local police received a *stolen goods* call from a man who just returned home from a business trip. His canoe is missing. The pvc gun was in the bottom of the canoe. Police claim he used the gun to ward off otters and coons. And here's the kicker. The two acre lot previously belonged to Olan and Ivy Chapman who let the canoe go with the property because of moving costs. Evidently, the movers wanted five hundred dollars to relocate the boats."

"Boats?" queried Josh Joyner.

"There's also a 16 horse outboard missing," said the female DPA director.

"Damn," said Josh Joyner watching the canoe disappear under the Packard Road overpass. He grabbed the two-way and barked, "Barricuda One, this is squad leader, over."

"This is Barricuda One," replied Agent Kramer.

"Follow that canoe," said Josh Joyner, "Zach, take the other chopper and give me air surveillance at

the mouth of this creek. As soon as I can collect Gold
berg, I'll take it from the ground."

Packard Road veers into Veterans Drive which
dead ends into Buffalo Avenue. Gill Creek follows the
same route, then continues on to the Niagara River.
Joyner and Goldberg reached the dead end to find an
empty canoe and no vigilante.

Agent Kramer and Agent Harrison emerged from
Barracuda One which now sat behind a silver guard rail.

"He's on foot,"   cried Harrison pointing to the
plant yard across the road,   "He's running between
storage tanks."

Josh Joyner brought up a aerial map on his two-
way. He pointed to a spot where Gill Creek runs under
Robert Moses Parkway, and empties into the Niagara
River.   Said Joyner,   "He's got to have the power boat
stowed here under this overpass. Now, Navy Island and
Grand Island lie just to the south. I want both choppers
to cover these two islands. One of them has to be his
destination. Agent Goldberg and I will try to beat this
guy to the boat."

Flying feet can sometimes outrun the speeding
motor car. Olan Chapman followed the creek bed
between storage tanks, and past a railroad spur that
served the chemical plant. The choppers were no

longer overhead. Thus, he lost no time seeking cover. He reached the Robert Moses parkway and splashed into the sludge water that puddled under the low overpass.

The 16 HP outboard waited at the far portal that opened into the Niagara River.

Chapman shivered his way through the icy murk and dragged the boat into flowing waters. His pursuers were nowhere in sight. Relief flooded in. Then, that *easy peaceful feeling* turned to anxiety when the motor wouldn't kick over.

He continued to fiddle with the pull choke as Josh Joyner pulled between medium trees on John Daly Boulevard.

"Reuben, this is the second time you've had to puke," said Josh Joyner as the rookie agent flopped back into the federal car, "We're losing our prey."

"I took in a lot of frigid water," said Reuben Goldberg, "I might be coming down with pneumonia. Does workman's compensation cover pneumonia?"

"Get Kramer on the horn," said Joyner.

"What's wrong with the heater?" asked Gold berg.

"Get Kramer on the horn," shouted Joyner, "We need that chopper back here !"

Moments later, pilot Richard Kramer came back with a code word that meant *no place to land the aircraft.* Joyner cursed and rammed the gas pedal to the floorboard. They merged into Robert Moses Parkway using the horn and no brakes. As they hit the 35mph zone, the speedometer peaked out. Medium-strip trees flew by like a picket fence. Agent Goldberg closed his eyes and grabbed the door strap. He advised Agent Joyner that the engine had a motor knock. Agent Joyner thanked Agent Goldberg for his concern.

The two agents reached the Gill Creek over pass as Olan Chapman went sea borne. A fading wake trailed the noisy out-board. Large black letters on the stern read *Bye Bye.*

Josh Joyner stood on the overpass bridge and swore softly. Agent Goldberg remained in the car, struggling with a frozen seat belt.

Then the unexpected.

"General," cried Joyner, "The boat's headed the wrong way !"

Navy Island and Grand Island lie south of the Gill Creek delta. The Falls spill north of the creek bed. When Chapman reached the channel's mid-point, he swung hard to the right and headed north.

"What the hell's he doing?' cried Joyner.

"He's committing suicide," replied Alexis .

"Damn!" cried Joyner, "He's a jumper. I never figured this guy to be a jumper!"

Said Alexis, "At the risk of breaking the chain of command, I think you better head out for Goat Island and try to stop the inevitable."

The twin helicopters returned from the Islands. They circled the Niagara River helplessly, as the stolen outboard churned toward the point of no return. When Olan Chapman reached Goat Island, he veered to the Canadian side, and headed toward the thundering Horseshoe Falls.

Suddenly, a third helicopter rose from the river basin and loomed through the steamy fog.

"Where the hell did that come from," cried Alexis Grumman following the action on the big screen, back at DPA Head quarters.

"Looks to be a home-grown swat team," replied co-pilot, Jocko Harrison peering through field glasses, "The chopper's non-tactical. Their ground support is camouflaged with yellow snow jackets. My guess is that somebody's got a police band radio."

The local swat team lined Goat Island's west coast, from Three Sisters Island to Terrapin Point. A few men held hand guns, most carried rifles. They were all volunteers from various neighborhood watches. The helicopter was non-tactical, indeed. The two-man chopper once belonged to a news station who used the open air, whirly bird to track down the scoop of the day. A man with a rifle leaned out the passenger doorway and opened fire on Chapman.

"Joyner, what's your ten-twenty !" screamed Alexis.

"I just pulled into Terrapin Point," said Josh Joyner stepping onto the icy parking lot. He grabbed his 9mm and looked up in time to witness the civilian chopper explode in mid-air. Multiple body parts dropped into the basin below. Cried Josh Joyner, "Dammit, the vigilante just shot down the chopper."

"Dammit," said Alexis Grumman.

"Dammit," said pilot Richard Kramer.

Swat members along the river bank opened fire on the 16 HP motor baot.

Chapman fired back.

Nearby tourists ran for cover.

"General," cried Josh Joyner, "We need a decision, here!"

Alexis Grumman popped a peppermint. She took a quick water drink and said, "Take him out."

QUANTUM ROOTS

Pilot Richard Kramer pulled up behind Olan Chapman's boat. Random shots from swat members had already disabled the outboard's engine, Water currents now pulled the boat along.

Chapman continued to fire toward the shoreline.

Kramer tilted the 60 caliber machine guns down ward. He lowered a face cover that was built into a sight helmet. A silhouette came up on a computer screen. When his target covered the cross-hairs, he pushed a safety button and squeezed the trigger.

Olan Chapman went over the falls in a cloudy mist, and a noisy rain of bullets.

CHAPTER 31

T'was the night before Christmas. Light snow fell on Powhatan Lake. Approaching carols filled the nippy air as Jeremy Wade climbed the porch steps to Cabin 18. The special agent paused to listen to the Grundy girls sing Silent Night. He was about to push a rusty chime button, when the third generation twins marched up and broke into a rendition of Little Drummer Boy.

"Hot chocolate for everyone !" cried Ivy Chap man swinging open the solid cabin door – and without missing a heartbeat, "That includes you, Agent Wade."

"Toby couldn't be here," chorused the Grundy Twins referring to their little brother, "He lost a front tooth and he can't whistle right."

The Powhatan Carolers featured three girls and three boys. The three girls sang. The three boys whistled. Almost everyone around the lakeside agreed the youths displayed extraordinary talent, and were undoubtedly headed for Radio City, or Nashville or maybe even America's Got Talent.

"Where's Janet Whithers?" asked Ivy Chapman who taught voice, coached elocution and selected the group's song list.

"Janet's at her grandmother's," said a Grundy twin, "And Bobby Fisher wet his pants and went home."

The last songbird was Timothy Ramsbottom who skipped this event to play video football.

"He's just mad because I shoved a snowball down his back," screamed Rebecca Grundy.

"I love working with kids," said Ivy Chapman as the twins disappeared down the street, "Olan and I never had any children and we always want what we don't have. . .I assume you're here on business."

"The proverbial pony topped my Christmas list," mused Jeremy, "Santa never brought me one, though."

Ivy Chapman opened a sack of Alfalfa oats. She filled several flat pans and fed her husband's growing herd of rabbits. She slipped out the bedroom door while the furry creatures ate. Making conversation she said, "Would you believe the freaking county tried to confiscate the rabbits. Fortunately, Chief Quayle has some connections at city hall."

"You must like rabbits," said Jeremy.

"Nobody likes this many rabbits," replied Ivy Chapman pouring chocolate milk into a giant punch bowl. She added rum and some tequila and said, "This is my version of the Mexican mud slide. Olan and I always share a mudslide on Christmas Eve. And since you don't seem to be leaving, you might as well stay and join us."

Ivy Chapman went on to explain that Olan Chapman never missed his Christmas Eve mud slide, regardless of marital conflict. True, their seven year hitch fell short of a Sunday cruise on still waters. Ivy would often blow up at any time of month. After which, Olan would disappear for days, sometimes weeks.

She recalled one Hyde Park incident when Olan went missing for a month. Ivy had run up a 300 dollar phone bill talking to her sister who lived in San Diego. Olan yanked the cord from the kitchen wall, and hurled the telephone through the plaster board.

On that particular Christmas Eve, Ivy found Olan half frozen in a pup tent just off the Robert Moses Parkway. His canoe sat perched on the river bank. His sleeping bag was wet, the zipper broken. They spent that night drinking mud slides, and rubbing more than noses to keep warm.

"Olan will be home for his mudslide," said Ivy a bit too firmly, "Make no mistake about that.. I know my Olan."

QUANTUM ROOTS

Elvis was halfway through his hit record *Blue Christmas*, when Ivy began to cry. And for a long hour, while snow fell, and Christmas carols faded, Special Agent Jeremy Wade sat on a quiet sofa, and held Ivy Chapman by the hand.

EPILOGUE

"Jeremy, step it up before we miss the boat."

"It's called a ship, Alexis."

"It might be a ship," said the DPA director dragging luggage from the taxi, "But if we are late for sign-in, we're going to miss the boat."

They checked in bags and were clearing customs when Jeremy Wade said, "I'm sorry you got canned, Alexis."

"I'm not canned," said Alexis Grumman, "Lieutenant Generals don't get canned. We get suspended without pay. After which, we take a cruise. Preferably, around the horn with Caribbean skies and bluewater beaches."

"I can't wait to see Cancun," said Jeremy dragging his foot cast up the gang plank.

They stopped inside the giant hull to greet the captain who wore a French emblem on his naval hat, and sounded English. He extended a handshake and exclaimed, "Lt General, Alexis Grumman, our honor to have you aboard, indeed."

"So much for incognito," said Alexis, "And the honor is ours, Sir."

"Can we expect a spot of espionage?" asked the ship's commander with a warm smile.

"I'm not in the spy business," replied Alexis, "My department deals more with strange people and odd events."

"Fascinating," said the salty captain weathered by sun and sea, "And the young man?"

"This is Agent Jeremy Wade," said Alexis, "He fractured an ankle stepping into a pot hole."

"By Jove," said the captain.

Jeremy Wade and Alexis Grumman sat on bar stools, waiting for luggage to catch up. Said Jeremy, "I'm with you on this. I want you to know that. The Director had no business canning you."

"I gave the kill order," said Alexis sipping rum and coke, "It goes with the territory."

"Alexis, the man was shooting people."

"It was my job to bring him in alive, Jeremy, "I failed in my mission."

"But he was shooting people !"

"Jeremy," said Alexis quietly as heads around the horseshoe bar began to turn, "Olan Chapman didn't kill anybody."

They were in the privacy of the elevator when Jeremy said, "I think you lost me, boss."

_____

"Jeremy, we recovered Chapman's gun belt not far from where we salvaged the boat. The gun belt was loaded with blanks. We never found the forty-five. However, not one swat team member suffered any gunshot wounds. Our films and our findings verify that Olan Chapman never hit anything or anybody."

"Alexis, he shot down the helicopter."

"No, he didn't," said the DPA director, "There were two men in that copter. Our medical examiner dug a rifle slug from one of the bodies. Somebody on the shoreline brought that copter down with an AK47."

"Who the hell would do that?" asked Jeremy.

"I don't know," replied Alexis, "It's no longer our problem."

They stood in a long corridor when Jeremy noticed all their luggage sat at just one state cabin door. Said the junior agent, "I thought you wanted two rooms,"

"Get your dreams out of your pocket, Jeremy," replied Alexis Grumman as she pulled the key from the door. Smiling slightly she added, "And don't count on seeing too much of Cancun."

*   *   *   *   *

Meanwhile in New York City, a white panel truck backed to the rear door of Club Cinema Cinder. The truck merely read *Delivery* because additional writing faded to oblivion. A blue clad driver jumped out. Bridge noise sounded over head. The Manhattan skyline loomed in the distance. The driver pushed a bell button marked for deliveries.

No answer.

He pounded on the steel roll-up door.

No answer.

Frustrated, the driver loaded four boxes onto a hand truck and legged it around the block. He ducked under the droopy awning of this Big Apple night spot and backed through the double front doors. Strobe lights and flashing bodies filled the dance floor. Here and there moved a person who looked almost human.

The delivery man stopped at stage front and motioned to Fatina. He held his ears and pointed to the boxes. The singer responded by pointing to a side door that led to the back. Seconds later, the singer and her cousin Caliph joined the driver, in a dimly lit room, loaded with costumes and sound equipment.

"I also have a message," said the driver handing over a long white envelope.

"I'm not expecting a message," said Fatina.

"Maybe it's from cousin Jamal," bubbled cousin Caliph, "Maybe the mission is over. Maybe the

Invisible Six are dead."

Fatina finished reading the coded message written in Arabic. Initial curiosity turned to rage. She pulled a drum from one of the delivery boxes. The driver grabbed the drug money due and disappeared.

Fatina threw the drum against a wardrobe closet. Thunder sounded. She grabbed a second drum. Cousin Caliph covered his ears. Fatina hurled the second and third drum at the first drum.

Hidden white powder flew everywhere as she screamed,   "Your stupid jackass cousin shot down the wrong helicopter !!!"

To Be Continued

QUANTUM ROOTS

Public domain information taken from the
Philadelphia Inquirer, Camden Courier Post
Burlington County Times, Bradenton Herald
and Online Encyclopedia, Wikipedia

Topographic data supplied by Google Maps.

Battle Of New Orleans excerpt adapted
from the 1959 song, Battle Of New Orleans,
sang by Johnny Horton and written by Jimmy
Driftwood. The Rockabilly hit won a 1960
Grammy Award, and eventually made the
Grammy Hall Of Fame.

Point Shooting techniques come from a handbook
written by Bobby "Lucky" McDaniel.

Cover Picture: Public Domain

Footnote:
As of this writing, the Maid Of The Mist boat tour of
Niagara Falls, lost their basin contract to Hornblower
Canada. Co due to competitive bidding. New takeover
is scheduled sometime in spring of 2014.

KYLE KEYES

Made in the USA
Columbia, SC
02 October 2020